"Planning on t ▮▮▮
a trip somew ▮▮▮

The sarcastic question startled
Caroline and she looked up to see
James standing in the doorway. She
fumbled with her suitcase, but it
refused to lock.

"Allow me." Her husband's long,
thin-fingered hands dealt with it
effortlessly. "So, you're moving in
with Redway?" He sounded remote as
though he were discussing a legal
problem with one of his clients. His
gray eyes watched her penetratingly.

She flushed deeply. "No! You
misunderstood...."

"You are a liar," he said through his
teeth. His hands fell on her shoulders,
gripping them tightly.

As his dark head came down,
Caroline groaned, "No, James!" She
could not bear the thought of
submitting to him with this terrible
gulf between them....

Other titles by

CHARLOTTE LAMB
IN HARLEQUIN PRESENTS

Other titles by

CHARLOTTE LAMB
IN HARLEQUIN ROMANCES

CHARLOTTE LAMB

dark dominion

Harlequin Books

TORONTO·LONDON·NEW YORK·AMSTERDAM
SYDNEY·HAMBURG·PARIS·STOCKHOLM

Harlequin Presents edition published March 1980
ISBN 0-373-10345-X

Original hardcover edition published in 1979
by Mills & Boon Limited

CHAPTER ONE

'You're going to be late,' said Caroline, glancing at the white face of the kitchen clock.

James lifted his black head and glanced at her round the edge of his copy of *The Times*. 'I shall be leaving in five minutes,' he said, and the precise, crisp tones of his voice jarred, as they had done for months.

She knew better than to argue. She went back into the kitchen and fidgeted about with the few items marring the spotless nature of the room. She heard his footsteps on the marble floor and turned her cheek for his brief kiss. The cold grey eyes inspected her as he touched his mouth against her cheek and a line etched itself between his arched dark brows.

'I can't stand that dress—it makes you look drab. Why don't you go into London today and buy yourself some new clothes?'

'Very well,' she said expressionlessly, raising her green eyes to his face.

His mouth compressed. 'It wasn't an order,' he snapped, 'merely a suggestion. It might cheer you up to do some shopping. God knows, you could do with it. I'm sick of seeing you wandering around this house like a ghost. You even dress the part.' His lips held a slight sneer. 'The actress in you, I suppose.'

That touched a thorn in her breast and her skin whitened. She looked away from him, her cheek a vulnerable curve.

'Hell,' he muttered, and walked out. Caroline heard the front door slam and then the sound of the car purring away down the drive.

It ought to have got better after six months, but daily it got worse. They lived together like two hostile strangers, barely speaking to each other when they were alone, their faces shuttered and icy. Sometimes she woke up in the night and reached out for him, tears coming to her eyes as she realised she was alone. It was at night that she was most vulnerable. She had never realised until six months ago how many terrors the night could hold. At first, the doctor had prescribed sleeping pills for her, and they had helped a good deal, but James had insisted that she stop taking them after a month. He said he did not want her to become dependent on them. The doctor had agreed with him, and to neither of them had she ever confessed that she had never had a full night's sleep since. The pattern varied. Sometimes she would sleep at once, only to wake up in the small hours, sweating and crying. Sometimes she would lie awake hour after hour, only to fall asleep towards dawn, exhausted and almost hallucinatory.

She broke off her thoughts to start the day's work, although there was little for her to do, since James insisted on having a daily woman to do the cleaning and the small, elegant Georgian house needed little extra work. While she was glancing around the sitting-room her eye fell on the wedding photograph displayed on the sideboard. She barely glanced at herself. Her gaze was fixed on James, lean and faintly smiling, his strong, austerely modelled features sharply outlined by the effect of the morning suit he wore. He had a Celtic face, long and lean, the jawline uncompromising, the mouth hard and straight. His eyes looked almost colourless in the sunlight.

Their first meeting had been typical of herself. She had literally run into him, flung to the pavement by the impact. That James should pursue it had been distinctly untypical. He had asked her out and she had accepted. Meeting the long stare of the icy grey eyes she had felt a curious spark leap between them and asked herself ruefully if she were not imagining it. Even then she had known that they came from different worlds.

He was a dozen years older than herself, a barrister, his world centred around the law courts, a man who had led a totally intellectual life, rational, clear-thinking, clever. On their first dinner date he charmed her with his wit and surprised her by his probing questions about herself. The evening had passed for her in a haze, where she poured out her life history and James listened, watching her flushed smiling face, his eyes moving from her green eyes to the wild haze of her red-gold hair and occasionally resting briefly on her mouth.

He had kissed her that first night, and it had shaken her to her roots. It was by no means her first kiss, but from the effect of it, it might have been. She had trembled like a leaf, her heart racing, and James, drawing back, had studied her almost clinically, as if to assess the result. Caroline could remember staring at the long, finely shaped hands as they curved around her hot face, her eyes on the wrists, focussing dimly on the dark hairs on his skin. Slowly her eyes had lifted to his face, touching the hard line of his mouth with incredulity. When she met his eyes her own mouth shook and as he bent to kiss her again she met his lips wildly, her arms going round his neck.

Even now the immediacy of his effect on her surprised her. She knew that logically they should have disliked each other. They were such different types of people, herself fire and air, James suggesting cold stone and water. They had nothing in common.

Except that from their first meeting desire had flamed between them almost visually.

Caroline had never in her life felt like that. She had been out with men before, but within hours of meeting James a passion for him was consuming her, and no words of common sense would have halted her flight into his arms. Within a week she would have gone to bed with him without a second's hesitation. When he made love to her she was incapable of thought, lost in a sensuous haze of pleasure, totally responsive to the hard, cool touch of his hands and mouth, and although James could show a poker face at times, he made no secret of the fact that he desired her. As time went on, his lovemaking deepened into naked hunger to which she responded wildly.

When he asked her to marry him, she did not hesitate. His proposal had a clipped, almost withdrawn ring which surprised her at the time, but when she accepted James drew a strange, fierce breath and swept her into his arms, kissing her throat, his body shaking. Caroline had been shaken by the moment herself.

At her wedding, she had felt possessively conscious of the quick, acquisitive looks James had got from some of her stage friends. Beneath that ice their feminine antennae picked up the fire, and Caroline had been both amused and bristling, and all the time she remembered her secret, obsessed waiting for the moment when they would be alone.

It was a struggle to recall the emotions she had felt that day. It might have been a hundred years ago, instead of merely two. An abyss lay between them now, but then she had only had to lay one finger on the back of his wrist in company to feel his pulse rate accelerate wildly, and throughout their wedding she had been permanently aware of his sensual consciousness of her beneath the cool, imperturbable mask he presented to the world.

Mrs Carter came into the room, shuffling in her old slippers. 'Anything special you want me to do today?'

Caroline started violently and turned a pale face towards her. 'What? Oh, no, thank you, Mrs Carter.'

The shrewd black eyes surveyed her unwinkingly. 'Look like a ghost, you do. Why don't you get some fresh air? Do some shopping.'

Remembering what James had said earlier, Caroline said vaguely, 'Yes, I think I will.' She thought of the journey up to London with a sigh. She rarely felt like making such an effort. She tried to remember when she had last gone up to town and couldn't fix on a date. The last six months slipped through her mind like water through a sieve. They had seemed endless. Time had ticked so slowly that she had felt each tiny second of it like a nail in her flesh. Yet they had all blurred together in her head like a fast-action film; grey, featureless, unmemorable.

'I think I'll go up to town,' she said.

Mrs Carter looked astonished, then grimly pleased. 'That's the ticket,' she said, nodding her wiry grey curls. 'Get out of here. That'll take you out of yourself.'

Out of myself, Caroline thought, as she sat in the London train, hearing the clicking of the wheels, the pneumatic wheeze of the doors whenever they stopped. What strange phrases people use! She often found herself examining the common small talk offered to her these days, the little clichés of life which people handed to one like crisps at a cocktail party, with a sage nod and an air of wisdom. Wouldn't it be wonderful if one *could* get out of oneself? She had been so sick of her own self for so long, and she remembered suddenly what fun it had been when she was at drama school to assume another identity for a while, to talk and behave like someone else, trying on emotions and backgrounds as if they were hats.

She made a face. If she started doing that now she would be locked up as a nut-case. Schizoid, definitely schizoid, she told herself in an imaginary magistrate's voice, pitying and reproving. Her eye caught a slight movement opposite and she looked across the carriage to find a young man eyeing her nervously. He had caught her face-pulling, she realised, and was speculating on her sanity. She was tempted to terrify him with her special gorilla face, but instead she got out a notebook and added a few squiggles to the brief list of things she wanted to buy.

Only two stops later, when the young man had left, did she realise that it was years since she had done her gorilla face. It had been the product of her days at drama school. One of their regular exercises was to imitate animals. It could be riotous fun and it was good practice. Her gorilla had been very popular with the other students. 'Watch it or you'll stay like it,' Jake had said, and she had mocked him, 'You're just jealous, Donald.' Because Jake's talent had lain in the area of imitating Donald Duck and their tutor had said once, 'A rather unoriginal ability, Redway. You'll never set the world on fire.' Yet it had been Jake who had gone on to become famous, a world star, while Caroline had left the stage after two cold years in rep and one brief season of glory in London. Jake had not come to her wedding. He had sent a telegram and a present. The telegram had made James's brows rise steeply and he had not put it with the others to be read to the wedding guests. She had giggled at it, but it had not amused James. I'll never forgive you, stop. I love you. Stop. Jake. James had crumpled it into a ball and thrown it into the waste-paper basket. Caroline had meant to rescue it later, but in the rush and excitement of her wedding day she forgot.

When she emerged into the daylight of Oxford Street it occurred to her that she had not thought of Jake once during the last six months. Odd how much distance can come between past and future. 'What is your history?' she murmured aloud to herself. 'A blank, my lord.'

Catching the quick glance of another shopper she

tried to assume a gormless expression. She really must stop the habit of talking to herself. It had grown on her during the months past. She had spent so much time alone in the house, rarely going out, refusing to accompany James to the many social functions he attended. He had tried, at first, to persuade her, but gradually his efforts had ceased. Nowadays he went his own way, leaving her to go hers, and suddenly she shivered, thinking of that, because she knew their marriage was tearing apart at the seams.

She wrenched her thoughts back to the subject of clothes and began to window-shop seriously. It was a bright June morning. The sun was high in the cloudless sky. A one-man band was banging and wheezing in the gutter, his cap on the pavement in front of him. She paused to drop a coin in his cap and he grinned at her round his mouth organ. 'Thanks, darling,' he said, and she grinned back, only realising as she walked away that it was the first spontaneous smile she had given anyone for months.

Like a child she rode up and down escalators in the great London stores, finding the noise and bustle of them exhilarating. She was carrying several large dress shop bags by now and juggling with them as she stepped on to an upper floor, she bumped into someone and dropped the lot.

'Oh, hell,' the other woman said, and her drawling voice made Caroline do a double take.

They recognised each other simultaneously. 'Caroline!'

'Maggie!'

For a moment they merely stood there, laughing, then Maggie stopped laughing and took a long, hard look at Caroline, her mouth turning down at the corners, her expressive, mobile face wry. 'My God, what's happened to you? If that's what matrimony does to a girl, thank God I stayed single!'

Caroline looked down at herself and saw herself with Maggie's eyes for a moment. 'I know,' she said, shuddering. 'I look awful.'

'Understatement,' Maggie said crisply. 'You look haggard and dreary and sick to death.' She slid a hand through her arm. 'Come and have a drink and spill your guts.'

Caroline found herself laughing again. That, she thought, was the sort of language which James detested, the attitude which had made Maggie persona non grata in their home. James had driven Maggie out of her life two years ago and only now did she realise how much she had missed her.

'I know a little place just around the corner.' Maggie always did. She had an unrivalled knowledge of London's little places, diving in and out of them like a rabbit through endless warrens. They found this one and Maggie summoned the waiter with a jerk of her frilly black head. When the drinks arrived, Maggie toasted her, the golden eyes warm. 'Here's to life in all its varieties,' she said, and Caroline remembered Maggie saying to her before the wedding, 'Leave the stage? You're crazy, girl.' And herself murmuring dreamily, 'Life has a variety of roles to offer.'

Over the rim of her glass Maggie surveyed her again from head to toe. 'Come on, cough ... how did James drag you down to this?'

'It isn't James's fault,' said Caroline. Her tongue moistened her lips. She had to say it. 'I miscarried six months ago,' she said. She spat it out quickly because if she said it slowly she might break down again and cry.

'Oh, I'm sorry,' Maggie said, sobering. 'Poor Caroline. What rotten luck!' She moved her head again and the waiter leapt up beside them like a genie brought by magic lamp. Caroline finished her drink and accepted another.

Maggie had always been the sort of luminous, sparklingly alive person who was needed to make any party come to life. Tall, very thin, with short black hair set in a flyaway tangle of ringlets which stood out around her hollow-cheeked face like sunrays, she magnetised people, and although she talked fast and funnily, she could listen and make people want to tell her their innermost secrets.

Caroline ought to have remembered Maggie's capacity for worming one's hidden thoughts out of one. Three drinks later she was telling Maggie the whole bitter story.

'We were very happy for the first year,' she said. 'It was perfect. We had a busy social life, but we were just as happy alone together, and we spent days putting the finishing touches to our house. James knew just what he wanted . . . he had this vision of the perfect home, very cool, very elegant. And it is, Maggie. You must see it.'

'I'll wait until I'm invited,' Maggie said tartly, because she knew James did not like her. She had been one of the stage friends whom he had wanted Caroline to give up. 'Tawdry,' he had called them. They did not mix with his friends. They laughed too much, talked too much and were too lively.

Caroline looked down into her glass, stirring the

contents with her little finger and sucking it. James objected to that habit, so she stopped, instinctively. 'But he began working for his silk and that meant he was spending more and more time away from home. He rang me every evening when he was on circuit, but I couldn't go with him, because it was dull and he couldn't concentrate with me there. So I decided to have a ...' She stopped, gnawing at her lower lip. 'A baby,' she said, screwing the word out in a harsh voice.

'Good idea,' said Maggie, watching her shrewdly.

Caroline smiled. 'James didn't think so. He didn't want children. He said: later, maybe. Not now. They would be disruptive. Children mean noise and mess.' She was talking in quick, clipped little sentences and it was the first time she had ever told anyone. It was hard to assemble all the facets of it. She took a deep breath. 'But I got pregnant,' she said hoarsely.

Maggie's golden eyes narrowed on her. 'Deliberately?' she asked quietly.

Caroline smiled. 'Oh, yes,' she said. 'I stopped taking the pill.'

'What did James say when you told him?'

'We had an icy row,' Caroline said. 'He was furious. I'd gone behind his back when I knew his views ... it ought to have been a shared decision, not a unilateral one, I had no right to force an unwanted child on him ...'

'God, the bastard,' Maggie said under her breath.

'No, he was right,' Caroline said. 'I had no business doing it.'

'Hell's teeth, it was done by then,' said Maggie disgustedly. 'And he had some part in the process, for God's sake. It was his damned baby.'

'I lost it at three months,' Caroline told her. 'Two days after our row, as it happens. Although it wasn't because of that ... I fell down the stairs, slipped on polished wood. James was very kind, very concerned.'

Maggie slowly looked her up and down. 'Someone has got to do a salvage job on you,' she said, changing the subject abruptly. 'Come on!'

Caroline let her pull her to her feet, frowning in slight bafflement, slightly muzzy with drink. 'Where are we going?'

'Here and there,' said Maggie. 'I know a little place just around the corner.'

Caroline was still giggling when they walked into the shadowy boutique and the owner stared at her in petrified revulsion.

'We want an image change,' Maggie told her.

'Dynamite, I'd say,' the owner muttered, but she dragged Caroline out of the plain grey dress she was wearing, its hem slightly sagging, its cut distinctly ugly, and forced her into a lustrous sea-green which clung to her body and gave her curves she had never known she possessed. Maggie pronounced herself satisfied with it and they took off again. In the same dazed state, Caroline found herself provided with shoes, lingerie and a hair-style. At this she demurred. 'James likes my hair the way it is,' she explained, and Maggie made a sick face.

'It makes you look like a timid dowager,' she said. 'Off with her head!'

Caroline emerged from the salon with a short, light cut, the red-gold curls falling like petals round her face, framing it, giving it a delicacy and emphasised bone structure it had never had before.

'My flat for lunch,' Maggie announced. 'I've got some salad and we've got to have a private chat before I let you vanish again.'

Over the salad, she said bluntly: 'I've given you a new outside. How about the inside? You can't go on brooding over the past, Caroline. It was rotten luck, but it's done with and you have your life to pick up. I've never cared much for James, but I did think he cared about you. What has he done about the way you were?'

'He tried,' Caroline said frankly. 'I can't explain what it was like, Maggie. A grey fog seemed to come down over me. I couldn't even see him through it. We drifted apart.' She looked down at her plate, poking the lettuce as though it harboured illegal inhabitants. 'We've been apart ever since it happened.'

Maggie pursed her lips in a silent whistle. 'I don't want to pry into intimate secrets, but by apart do you mean ... ?'

Caroline shrugged. 'Yes, we don't sleep together.'

'Your idea? Or his?'

'Mine,' said Caroline reluctantly. 'Although it was something which just happened. I couldn't sleep after I lost the baby, so I started sleeping in a room of my own, and I just went on doing it.'

'James didn't try to stop you?'

'Not at first, then there was a time ... but I got hysterical when he touched me. We had a terrible row and I said some very bitter things.'

'You were still blaming him for the baby?'

Caroline sighed. 'Yes, although with my rational mind I knew it wasn't his fault, but I couldn't get it out of my mind that he hadn't wanted the baby. I felt ... stupid though it sounds ... that he had killed it.'

Maggie winced at the white misery in her face. 'And you told him so?'

Caroline lifted stricken eyes. 'Yes.'

Maggie whistled. 'That must have been the row to end all rows!'

'It was horrific,' Caroline agreed.

'And since then?'

'It's been like living in the frozen wastes of Antarctica,' Caroline said, trying for lightness.

Maggie finished her meal in silence and pushed the plate away. 'Caroline, it can't go on ... you've got to ask James for a fresh start. Talk to him the way you've talked to me, calmly, without bitter recriminations.'

Caroline nodded. 'Yes,' she said, 'I know. I have tried, but there's this great hole in the ground between us and every time I try to talk to him I fall into it.'

The golden eyes half closed in thought. 'I've an idea. I'm having a party tonight. Why not come and bring James?' Maggie's smile broke suddenly. 'Yes, I'd forgotten ... Jake will be there! Every time I run into him he asks about you. He'd love to see you again—you two were always as close as Siamese twins. Caroline, you must come.'

'I don't know.' James had never liked her stage friends or her stage parties. His sort of party was the opposite of theirs—dignified, witty, leisurely.

'It would give you a chance to break out of that vicious circle of yours,' Maggie pointed out.

'Yes.' She could see that. It would certainly be

different and she needed light, colour, noise at the moment. Coming to London and meeting Maggie had shown her that.

'I'll try,' she said, nodding. 'I promise, I'll try ... what time?'

'Any time.' Maggie grinned at her. 'You know how it goes ... once it starts, our parties go on all night and end with breakfast in the morning.'

'For those able to face food,' Caroline agreed, laughing back.

'There is that.' The returning grin was infectious. She had forgotten how Maggie could lift the spirits. Just being in her company for a few hours had been a tonic. She glanced at her watch. 'If I can catch James at his chambers I can stop him coming home. Once he's in the house it will be a difficult job getting him out of it again.' In the evenings he sat in his study, his black head bent over piles of papers, the circle of his lamp excluding him from her. They rarely spent the evening together now. He worked until late at night and Caroline went to bed early with a brief word and a brush of cold cheeks.

'That's a good idea,' said Maggie. 'You could ring him from here.'

Caroline fidgeted with her fingers, head bent. 'I'd better go there in person. A telephone message wouldn't work.' She was going to have to beg to get him here. James was not going to be easy to persuade.

Shrewdly, Maggie said, 'I've never understood what brought you two together. Chalk and cheese. I grant you, he's got sex appeal, but he wouldn't turn me on ... too much granite under that smooth suit.'

'It's just one of those things,' Caroline said, sighing.

'How did you meet him? I never knew.'

'Literally ran into him,' she said. 'In the street.'

Maggie's brows lifted ironically. 'And he asked for a date? I don't believe it—James Fox?'

Caroline laughed. 'He made it sound very reasonable. He'd knocked me to the pavement and he insisted on buying me a drink to help me over the shock.'

'It sounds like him. And one thing led to another?'

'We were married so fast I barely knew what was happening,' Caroline confessed. James had been a stranger from another planet, knowing nothing of her wild, cheerful world, and she had been so mad about him that she had barely noticed as he quietly peeled her away from her friends, the ironic lift of his dark brows enough to curtail any meeting with one. For a very long time she hadn't needed anyone but him, anyway. The honeymoon period had lasted for months, their idyllic isolation contenting both of them. Only when James turned back to his work and withdrew from her did she grow lonely, realising how she missed her own friends.

'People still ask where you've vanished to,' Maggie said, eyeing her. 'You dropped out of sight without a trace.'

'Marriage does that,' Caroline shrugged.

'It sounds to me,' Maggie murmured, 'as though there's more to your depression than the loss of your baby.'

Caroline flushed and made a wry face. 'I was never very good at being alone.'

'You were a little firework when I knew you,' said Maggie, warmth in her voice. 'Bright and lively. You should never have given up your career.'

'That was the way he wanted it.'

'Chauvinist!'

'James invented the word,' Caroline smiled. She stood up. 'I'll take a taxi to his chambers. He'll probably be in court, but I can see Withers.'

'Withers?' Maggie giggled.

'His chief clerk. He's a kind little man, bland as milk.' Caroline looked around. 'Could I telephone for a taxi?'

'I'll get you one,' said Maggie, picking up the phone.

She kissed Caroline as the taxi drew up in the street below. 'Now, don't forget ... be there, to-night. There'll be a crowd of people you know and some you don't—it'll be a good party, Caro.'

In the taxi Caroline rehearsed the way she would ask James, her fingers writhing together in anxious preparation. I'm frightened of him, she thought, and the thought made her flinch. What's gone wrong between us? I wasn't frightened in the beginning. It's grown on me with time.

The crowded chaos of West End traffic thinned out as she entered the city, the taxi picking up speed as it shook itself free of other cars. Offices and tower blocks gave way to the dignified grey stone of Lincolns Inn Fields, the trees and grass of the gardens brightening the sky. The taxi drew up outside James's chambers and she paid the driver, turning on the pavement to stare up at the flat windows.

She took a deep breath. No doubt he would be in court, but she could get a message to him, asking him not to go home but wait for her at his chambers.

She went into the building and picked her way up the stairs, their old wood creaking under her feet.

Withers was not in his office. A girl in a red dress sat there, typing, her face sullen. She looked at Caroline with a cross mouth. 'Can I help you?'

'I want to speak to Mr Withers,' Caroline said.

'He'll be back in a minute,' the girl told her, returning to work without a smile.

Caroline stood there, glancing around the room, then her ears picked up a familiar voice. James! She turned and walked out, moving down one of the corridors, up a short uneven flight of stairs. He was not in his own office, she realised. The sound of his voice came from another one. She paused at a door, listening, hesitating. Should she knock? Or wait until he was free? He might be with an important client and she did not want to prejudice her chances of getting him to Maggie's party by making him angry by bursting in on a vital meeting.

Trying to estimate how important the conversation was, she bent her head against the door, listening.

James's voice came to her clearly then, and her body froze as she heard what he was saying.

'I should never have married her!' His voice was bitter, harsh. She heard the slam of a hand on a desk. 'It was madness!'

'Couldn't you talk to her, James?' The other voice was feminine, clear, assured, and Caroline did not recognise it.

'How the hell can I at the moment? It would be brutal to force that sort of discussion on her at present.'

'James, it's six months since she lost the baby! Surely she must have got over that by now.'

'No.' James sounded muffled now, his voice distant.

'Have you tried?'

He laughed roughly. 'My nerve fails me every time I consider it.' He moved and Caroline heard every step he took on the carpet, his soles brushing the pile. White-faced, she stared at the door.

'I'm going out of my mind,' he said raggedly. 'Linda, I can't even concentrate on work while things are like this between us ... something has got to give or I'll crack.'

'James ...'

The husky note in the woman's voice brought Caroline's head up, her eyes wide and shocked. She could not see the other woman's face, but she knew what she was hearing.

'We'll find a way, James,' the woman was whispering. 'I promise you, we'll find a way.'

Caroline had to see her. She had to see them both with her own eyes and face the facts which were staring her in the face. Her hand touched the door handle, slipped off it because her palm was slippery with sweat. She grasped it again and opened the door.

Across the room she saw James's lean, dark back, his head bent. A woman was in his arms. Caroline could not see her face, only the sleek brown wreaths of her hair, but she did not need to see any more. She looked at the desperate clutch of those white hands on James's shoulders, saw the lifted head and heard the kiss.

She closed the door on a reflex movement and

walked round a corner to lean on the wall in an attitude of pain, her face in her hands.

Dimly she heard the door open again.

'Someone came in,' James said sharply.

'You imagined it,' the woman was reassuring him.

'No,' he said, certain.

'Does it matter?' The woman sounded half amused. 'Good heavens, James, we were committing no crime!'

'It might have looked ...' James broke off. 'Forget it.'

The door closed again and Caroline fought down the agony which was draining her. She couldn't walk out of the building yet. Her face would be too revealing and Withers might be back. She had to pass him to leave. When her face was calm she walked back to his office, treading quietly past James's door. The girl sat there typing, but there was no sign of Withers, and the girl gave her no glance, indifferent.

She walked through the dulling streets for hours, her body weary and her mind tortured. She had guessed now who the woman was, she should have guessed at once. James had mentioned his new partner, Linda Blare, and she had never listened with real attention, but now she sought her memory for clues which might betray the relationship to her in hindsight. 'A clever lady,' James had said with amusement when he first mentioned her. 'Cool as a cucumber and as sharp as a needle. We're lucky to get her.' The other partners were all men. Linda was related to the head of the chambers—her uncle, Caroline seemed to remember. She had joined the firm about a year ago.

A year.... just about the time when their marriage began to contract and show signs of strain. The time when James had coldly refused to have a child. Because he did not want to cement their marriage? she asked herself now. Had he merely felt that marrying Caroline had been a mistake?

She stood on the embankment looking down into the leaden Thames. It had begun to rain. Her bright red-gold hair darkened with it, her face grew wet. She stared at the river and her hands clenched on the grey stone parapet.

A step slowed beside her and a hand fell on her arm. 'All right, miss?'

She started, looking round into a policeman's kind, shrewd watchful face.

'Oh ... yes, thank you,' she said, stammering a little.

'Getting wet, aren't you?' he asked, still watchful.

She forced a faint smile. 'A little ... nasty weather.'

A taxi was cruising past. Caroline saw the 'for hire' sign glowing and hailed it, giving the policeman a quick smile.

Instinct made her give Maggie's address. She could think of nowhere else to go. The idea of returning to the house she had shared with James was anathema.

Maggie opened the door and stared, brows rising. 'You're back quickly. And soaked to the skin, I see.' Then her voice altered. 'Caro? My God, what's wrong with you?'

Caroline smiled wildly. 'I'm fine, just fine, absolutely fine.'

Maggie put an arm around her waist and guided

her to a chair, pushing her into it. A moment later a glass was pushed into her hand. 'Drink that.'

'I don't . . .'

'Drink it!'

Caroline drank obediently and felt the warmth flickering along her veins. She raised a white face and gave Maggie a dry smile. 'Really, I'm okay.'

'Tell me about it,' Maggie commanded.

'No!' The tone was fierce. She could not have mentioned what she had overheard and seen to anyone.

Maggie eyed her, chewing her lower lip. 'But I take it that James is not coming to my party?'

Caroline laughed. 'You take it correctly,' she said in a voice bordering on hysteria.

'Well, you are,' Maggie said firmly.

The last thing Caroline wanted was to go to a party. 'I'd love to, Maggie, but . . .'

'You need it,' Maggie told her, taking her chin and grimacing at her. 'When you walked in here just now you were worse than when I saw you earlier today . . . you left here as bright as a button. You came back looking as if someone had put you through a mangle. Damn James. You, my girl, are staying for my party.'

CHAPTER TWO

'You can help me with the drinks,' Maggie said later, as they waited for the first guests to arrive. They had laid out all the food on a long table, quiches, paella, curried patties, little bowls of other food, the usual party impedimenta. Maggie had done what she called a 'rescue job' on Caroline, brushing her new hair-style into shape, doing her face with little pots of cream and a dressing-table covered with make-up. The flat looked immaculate and strangely empty as it waited for people to fill it.

Caroline looked at herself in the mirror, her face wry, seeing the curved reflection of her body in the sea-green dress. Outwardly she looked fine. Nobody was going to guess how she felt inside; she would see to that.

The door bell went and Maggie grinned. 'The war's on!'

Caroline knew the first arrival and there were loud exclamations of surprise and pleasure. She quickly framed a brief résumé of her life over the past two years, leaving out all mention of the miscarriage, making it sound gay and happy. Maggie's golden eyes met hers drily as she spoke, but she said nothing.

An hour later the room was full, the air thick with smoke and loud with voices. Caroline circulated with food and drink, smiling, talking. She had gone through her little patter many times over, giving it a gloss which disguised the hidden truths. People asked the same questions, took the same answers with complete acceptance. It was beginning to sound so good she believed herself.

She went into Maggie's little kitchen to find new supplies and was rummaging in a cupboard, her head inside it, when hands encircled her waist, making her squeak.

'Got you!' said a voice so strangely familiar that her heart turned over.

She spun, eyes wide, laughing. 'Jake!'

'You dirty rat, you,' he said in his duck voice, hands squeezing her waist.

'Jake,' she said again, and found nothing else she could say, because it was such a pleasure to see him again. Seeing Maggie had been wonderful, but although she and Maggie had been very close, Jake had been her closest friend and ally.

'Marry Freddie, would you?' he asked, and she looked puzzled, then laughed, tracking down the quotation to *Pygmalion*.

'I planned to fly back from the States and do a spot of quiet assassination,' he told her. 'But if James Fox was really what you wanted I decided I'd grin and bear it.'

'You've got to the top, Jake,' she said, congratulating him.

'Top of the world, Ma,' he said lightly. He had always had a passion for James Cagney. They had spent a lot of evenings at the National Film Theatre watching old movies, eating popcorn and peanuts.

James would never have put up with the sort of film she and Jake enjoyed. He liked intellectual stuff, Chekhov, Ibsen. It reminded her, and she looked at Jake.

'You rang the bell with your run in *A Month in the Country*.'

'Flattery,' he said beatifically, 'I love it.'

'You always did.'

'Like a bath in warm treacle,' he added.

'Ugh!'

He grinned at her, his handsome-ugly face alight. It was, she thought, a memorable face; the bones large and angular, the brown hair dishevelled in a wildly appealing fashion, the eyes as bright as blue glass under their comical brows. Thick, bristling and black, those brows had made his face unmistakable. Cartoonists seized upon them eagerly. They were his personal signature now.

'What was it like making a film?' she asked.

'Dead boring,' he said. 'God, I read some books, Caroline. Waiting, waiting ... like being at Heathrow when the ground staff are on strike. I even read *War and Peace*.'

'You must have been desperate.'

'I thought of you,' he said abruptly, looking into her face.

She met the look with smiling eyes. 'With all those glamour girls around? Full of them, the film world.'

'Glamour girls!' His snort was contemptuous.

She mocked him softly, 'Don't tell me they could resist your boyish charm?'

He gave her an insolent look. 'I won't,' he said.

'You could pick and choose, I suppose?' She was still mocking, her lashes lowered and her eyes gleaming through them.

'Jealous?' Jake's smile was sardonic.

'Madly,' she said.

He put a finger on her cheek and drew it down slowly to the corner of her mouth. 'I've missed you.'

Caroline nodded, not answering, not disputing, She had missed him. For three years they had been part of each other and James had cut them off deliberately. She thought of Jake's wedding telegram and sighed.

'You never did meet James,' she said.

Jake's wide, strong mouth hardened. 'Just as well,' he said.

She looked up at him. 'Why?'

'I'd have punched his handsome nose for him,' Jake told her.

She did not take his professed jealousy seriously. There had never been anything romantic between herself and Jake, more of a brother-sister relationship than anything else. This was a game Jake played supremely well. In the old days he had used her to keep other girls at bay. His open, loud adoration of her had been a useful weapon against other females and she had permitted it without question.

Jake tightened his hands on her waist, lifting her to the kitchen table as lightly as though she were a child. He joined her, swinging his long legs. She looked him up and down, inspecting him properly for the first time.

'You've changed,' she commented.

'So have you,' he said, his eyes narrowed on her. The long glance lingered on her soft, rounded breasts beneath the fine sea-green silk. 'You weren't that shape last time I saw you.' He made a lecherous face. 'Marriage has improved your potential.'

She giggled. 'Thanks.' She had never noticed it herself until now, but in fact her body had altered during the two years with James, she realised.

'You were a skinny little monstrosity when we first met,' he said. 'You've matured interestingly.'

'It's mutual,' she said, glancing sideways at him. His shoulders had broadened since they last met. It gave the long line of his waist and hips a tapered, lean power she could imagine made him irresistible to the women he met. She had read of his sexual exploits in the gossip columns. 'You got quite a reputation for yourself over in the States,' she said. 'Women coming out of your ears.'

He leered at her. 'I didn't waste my opportunities,' he agreed wickedly.

'Vile creature!'

He grinned. 'What about you? Marriage up to your expectations?' The bright eyes ran over her again. 'It's done something for you, I'll say that. Were you always this sexy?'

'You mean you never noticed?'

The light banter was easy to fall back into, as if they had never been apart.

'Oh, I noticed,' he said, giving her a sideways look. 'It was you who didn't.' His eyes grew serious. 'Why did you vanish from sight, Caro? Too preoccupied with your husband?'

'Something like that.' She looked away, veiling her expression.

'Two years,' he said softly. 'Two damned years ... don't do that to me again.'

Maggie came into the room and glanced at them expressionlessly. 'Having fun?' she asked lightly.

'Catching up,' Jake told her, swinging his legs. 'A lot of water under bridges to remember.'

'You are the star of the evening,' Maggie murmured. 'Could it wait until later? People are waiting to talk to you.'

'Let them wait,' he shrugged, and the arrogance was new, making Caroline look at him sharply.

Maggie sighed. 'Come on, Jake. Don't go all big star on us!'

His face hardened and the blue eyes were cold. 'What?'

Maggie's face flushed. 'We all know you're God's gift to the stage, but I'd be grateful if you'd condescend to come down off Olympus for one night.'

Jake's eyes flashed and Caroline laid a hand on his arm. The muscles tensed under her fingers and he turned his brown head, shooting her a quick look.

'Maggie's right—we can talk later.'

Her eyes pleaded with him and a curious look came into his face. He sat, staring at her, his brows meeting.

Unconsciously she had used the humble, begging voice she had grown used to using to James. The flint-like obduracy of his character made it necessary and the change in her had been so gradual that she only realised it under Jake's shrewd, narrow-eyed stare.

He dropped down off the table and lifted her down, too, his hands hard on her waist. 'You're not planning to skip off early?'

She thought of returning to the cold, empty elegance of her home and her face stiffened into a mask. 'No,' she said. 'I'm not in a hurry to go.'

'Stay the night,' Maggie said quickly, watching her. 'There's a spare room.'

'Thanks, I'd like to,' she said.

Jake nodded. 'Then we've a date for later,' he told her. He turned to Maggie. 'Lead me to your lion-eaters,' he said.

'Conceited bastard,' said Maggie, mouth wry.

He laughed, following her back to the party, and Caroline went on gathering together the food she had come in search of earlier. She went back to the party herself and saw Jake, surrounded by a circle of faces, his strong face amused. He was, she saw, enjoying himself. She watched him flirt openly with a pretty blonde, his lashes brushing his brown cheeks. The girl was blatant in her eagerness and Caroline guessed that this was a pattern often repeated. Jake had reached the top all right!

Maggie sidled up to her and took a stick of celery from a jar. 'He's giving a great performance,' she said drily.

'Doing you proud,' Caroline agreed, and they grinned at each other.

'He's a fine actor,' Maggie admitted, as though to wipe out any suspicion of professional jealousy. 'He deserves his success.'

'Strange, though,' Caroline murmured. 'Remember what a fool he could be at drama school? If anyone was playing around it was always Jake. I never thought he was really serious about acting.'

'Maybe he's a better actor off stage as well as on than we realised,' said Maggie, glancing at her oddly.

Caroline emptied the ashtrays and removed a pile

of dirty glasses, then went into the kitchen to wash them. A young man in cords and a white sweater followed. 'Need any help?'

'Thanks,' she said, smiling.

They worked in harmony. 'Actress?' he asked, looking her up and down.

'No,' she said, faintly rueful.

He looked surprised. 'Friend of Maggie's?' Maggie didn't know anyone outside the theatre. Her whole life was bounded by it.

'Yes,' Caroline said.

Again the quick look. 'Model?'

She smiled, shaking her head.

'You ought to be,' he said, the tone slightly insinuating. 'You could be very successful. Want any introductions? I could get you some work.'

Caroline gave him a cool look. 'No, thank you. I'm married.'

He backed away as though she had slapped him. 'Well, glad to be of help any time.' He vanished as though in fear of his life and she grinned to herself. A try-on, she thought. It was a long time since anyone had tried to date her with that sort of line, and it was amusing.

Maggie came in and made a face at her. 'Stop ducking in here and join the rest of us ... you're here to enjoy yourself, not work!'

Caroline let her pull her back into the throng and smiled at people, talked, made gay small talk, listened to theatrical shop. She found herself back to back with Jake at one moment. They touched and glanced round at each other. He winked. The blonde was still hanging on his arm and he was making no effort to dislodge her. Caroline's eyes flicked from her to Jake and she smiled pointedly at him, turning away.

She began to feel she had never been away. At first it had been difficult to put aside the memory of James with another woman in his arms, but now she was doing it without effort. Whenever the sharp little picture flashed into her head she pushed it away and smiled even more.

The party began to die at around two. People drifted away, the air grew clearer and the music was turned down. A few guests shuffled around to it, dancing sleepily, now that there was room to move. Jake detached himself from the blonde and came over to her.

'Dance?'

She looked at him in surprise, then over at the blonde, who was looking at her with open jealousy.

'I don't want my eyes scratched out. Go back to Goldilocks.'

Jake didn't answer. He put his arm round her waist and pulled her close. She followed him round the room, her hand on his broad shoulder.

He put his cheek against the light feathers of her hair. 'Maggie tells me your marriage is on the rocks.'

Caroline stiffened, falling over his feet. 'She had no right ...'

He looked down at her, his face hard. 'We're your oldest friends, Maggie and I. She had every right. We're concerned.'

'It's none of your business!' Pain made her voice harsh.

'From what Maggie told me, James Fox is a swine.'

'I shouldn't have told her anything. I didn't think

she'd go around repeating what I said to every Tom,
Dick and Harry.'

Jake's arm tightened, hurting her. 'Are you *trying* to insult me, Caro?'

Her eyes flickered up to meet his and saw the
anger in his face.

'I'm sorry,' she muttered.

'So I should damned well hope.'

'But my marriage is a private affair.'

'You told Maggie,' he pointed out. 'Why exclude
me?'

Her face flushed under the probe of his eyes. 'I
was distraught when I talked to Maggie. I needed a
shoulder to cry on, I suppose.'

'Use mine,' he said.

She smiled. 'It's different.'

'We were always closer than you and Maggie,' he
bit out. 'Aren't we friends any more, Caro?'

James had not liked Maggie, but she knew very
well that he would dislike Jake even more if he met
him. She smiled wryly. 'You made a distinct impression on James with that telegram of yours,' she told
him.

He shot her a shuttered look. 'Made him jealous,
did it?'

Something in his voice made her look at him
closely. 'Jake! Was that deliberate?' It had never
occurred to her before. She had taken it as one of
Jake's jokes. James had been furious with it, but
they had forgotten it in the heady days of their
honeymoon.

'I thought I'd give him something to think about,'
Jake shrugged. 'Why did you marry an outsider,

Caro? Suddenly, out of the blue, while I was on the other side of the world?'

'If I told you, I suspect you wouldn't understand,' she said.

'Why the hell shouldn't I?' He was belligerent now.

'Love,' Caroline said sadly. 'I fell in love, Jake.'

He was silent, staring over the top of her head. 'And now?'

She closed her eyes, shivering. 'God knows.'

'You're out of your depth,' Jake said. 'Maggie thinks you should leave him and come back to us.'

'Maggie thinks!' She was breathless with offence. 'I wish she'd keep her thinking to herself!'

'You belong on the stage. You were a damned good actress.'

'I never got anywhere.'

'You gave up too soon. When I left you were nicely established in a good part at the Quality.'

'It wasn't bad,' she admitted, remembering the excitement and heady delight of those days.

'Why not try again?' he asked, looking down at her. 'It's your world as much as it's mine. We'd both help, Maggie and I. I know a lot of people now. I could drop your name in some ears.'

She laughed. 'God, I didn't realise I had some lofty influence!'

He grinned, relaxing. 'Well, realise it now. Be frank, Caroline. Do you want to get back into the theatre or not?'

She thought of James with the woman in his arms. He wanted to end their marriage. He saw it as a mistake, and maybe he was right. They had not been happy together for a year and the nervousness with which she regarded him did not make for a good relationship.

Jake was watching her, trying to read her face, and she looked up at him, her features torn by confused emotions.

'I don't know.'

'Sleep on it,' he said, with a satisfied little smile. 'I'll see you tomorrow morning. I've an idea of a small part in a television series which you could audition for.'

'Oh?' Her pulses picked up at the casually spoken words. Colour ran into her cheeks and he grinned down at her, amused.

'That woke you up with a vengeance, did it?'

'What part?' she asked eagerly.

'I'm doing a series on Napoleon,' he told her. 'They're looking for a Josephine. The way the series is written, it's only a few lines ... the emphasis is on the military side of his character. I can't promise they'll even consider you for the part, mind, but you could audition.'

'If you insist,' she said shrewdly, watching him.

He was a big name now. He could manipulate things like that. He might not be able to guarantee her the part, but he could certainly guarantee that they would look at her to please him.

Jake stood still, shifting his hand around her chin. 'Shall I get that audition for you?'

Caroline searched for an answer, not certain what it should be. If James did want a divorce, she had to have a future, a life without him. She had missed her friends, her familiar shop talk, the whole obsessive inward-looking world of the theatre.

'Yes,' she said suddenly, impulsively. 'Thank you, Jake.'

His face had a strange, hard triumph in it. 'Right,' he said. He glanced across at the waiting blonde, her face sulky. 'I'd better get back to her before she loses patience and runs out on me.'

Caroline laughed. 'Do that.'

'See you,' he said, and strolled across to the other girl. Her face brightened at his approach and a smile dawned on her seductively pink mouth. Caroline watched them with wry amusement. Jake had it made, she thought. One look and they all toppled. She did not remember him as a womaniser, but he plainly enjoyed his role now.

That night Maggie settled her in the spare bedroom, lending her a daring black nightie with red lace threaded through the neckline. 'Oh, I must ring James!' Caroline exclaimed, stricken as she realised she had not remembered it before.

'At three in the morning?' Maggie raised her eyebrows. 'Now that I wouldn't advise, honey. If he has to get up early to shoot off to court he won't thank you.'

'No.' Caroline bit her lip. 'Maybe you're right.' Then, paling, 'I wonder what he thinks I'm up to.'

'Leave it until the morning,' she was told, and the light was snapped off firmly.

She fell asleep almost at once, but before dawn she woke up with a start, tears in her eyes, and this time she knew what she had been dreaming about— she could still see them, the woman's head raised, James bending over her, hear the agonised murmur of his voice as he muttered, 'God, I can't take it any more.'

They had lost each other somewhere along the way, she thought. James had loved her once, she did not doubt that, but they had been from such different worlds, their natures utterly opposed. James made his living with that hard, cold brain; he was a dangerous opponent in a court, his tongue cruel and icy, his eyes like piercing steel across the room. She had once been to see him work. Never again. It had frightened and upset her. The tall, white-wigged stranger standing there had been a nightmare figure to her. It had been after that, she realised, that she had grown frightened of him. He had begun to use his court voice on her, his tone cold and clear, his eyes penetrating. She had responded by shrinking from him.

Maggie was right. The loss of her baby had been the final straw in what had happened. She and James had been tearing apart long before that.

Until the tragedy of her miscarriage, though, they had still had one safe meeting ground—their bed. The sensuous hunger of their love had continued to exist there. James had always been a passionate lover. She closed her eyes, wincing. So long ... it was so long since he had held her in his arms.

They had done each other terrible damage. She had only realised what he had done to her when she saw Maggie again and was brought face to face with the difference in herself since they last met. James had taken her lively, extrovert personality and reshaped it to his own ends, but in the process he had destroyed all that was real and alive about her. She had grown quiet and subdued, till at last she had withdrawn from life altogether.

What damage she had done James had been less

obvious. That she had done some she had realised when she heard the agony in his voice that morning. She had hurt him and she bitterly regretted it.

There was only one thing to be done about it.

'I must divorce him,' she thought aloud, her voice shaking, and the sound of her voice startled the silence in the little room. She closed her eyes, drained, and slowly fell back into sleep.

When she woke up it was broad daylight and Maggie was thrusting a tray on to her lap. 'Tea and toast,' she said. 'I'm off for a rehearsal. See you this afternoon?'

Caroline met the questioning glance of her golden eyes and smiled at her. 'Afraid I'm going to become a permanent inhabitant of your spare room, angel?' She used the old endearment lightly. They had used such names freely once. Honey, angel, darling ... meaningless yet full of meaning.

'It's yours for as long as you want it,' said Maggie. The straight look she gave Caroline was calm. 'You could do with a break.'

'Jake mentioned something about an audition,' Caroline told her.

Maggie's eyes widened. 'For you?'

'Possibly.'

'And you accepted?' Maggie was smiling again, broadly.

'I think so,' Caroline said, grimacing. 'I was a trifle dazed by then. Jake was very persuasive.'

'Tell me all about it when I get back,' said Maggie, looking at her watch. 'I'm late. I must fly or I'll get an earful of choice epithets from Baldy Longword.'

'Is he producing you?' Caroline was envious. He

was a respected figure, his fringed bald head monk-like, his eyes clever and shrewd. 'Lucky you!'

'Not,' said Maggie ruefully, 'if I'm late!'

When she had gone, Caroline nibbled the toast and drank some tea, then looked at the clock and leapt out of bed, realising she still hadn't rung James.

He wouldn't be at home now, she thought. He would probably be in court. She rang his chambers and Withers answered. When she identified herself his voice deepened. 'Oh, Mrs James!' He always called her that, as though she were the wife of the eldest son. 'Mr James has been very worried about you . . .'

'I stayed the night with a friend after a party,' she told him. 'I'm afraid I forgot the time. You know how it is . . . I didn't want to wake my husband at a late hour.'

'He didn't sleep,' Withers said reproachfully. 'He's been out of his mind about you . . . rang the police, the hospitals . . .'

She paled. 'Oh, no!' Why hadn't it occurred to her that James would be so worried? She had behaved irresponsibly, vanishing without a word to anyone. 'Is he in court now?'

'No,' Withers said. 'He's at home, waiting for you.'

Caroline rang off quickly and rang James. The receiver lifted before the first ringing tone had ended. 'James?' she murmured nervously.

There was a silence which seemed to her to last for ever.

'Where the hell have you been?' The question burnt her ear and she jumped.

Her words fell out in stammered incoherence. 'I'm sorry I didn't ring. I went to a party ... I forgot the time and it was so late I stayed the night.'

'Where? Who with?' he asked harshly. 'Where are you?'

She hesitated, afraid to mention Maggie's name and make him even more angry. 'I ... the ... friend who gave the party ... it was easier than getting a taxi all the way home and waking you up.'

'What's the address?' he asked.

Automatically she gave it to him. 'James, I do apologise. I realise it must have worried you, but I'm all right. It was thoughtless of me not to let you know.'

'Oh, you've realised that?' He sounded bitterly sarcastic. 'Stay there, I'll come and get you.'

'No,' she said quickly. 'I ... I thought I'd stay a few days. You're very busy and I haven't much to do at home. You won't mind if I'm away for a little while, will you?'

The silence again, but she could hear him breathing, the sound thick and irregular.

'You'd better get off to work,' she said with a nervous little laugh. 'Poor Withers is frantic. I'm sorry to have caused all this trouble.'

'Are you?' He sounded distant now, his voice icing over. 'A pity you didn't think of that before. Goodbye, Caroline.'

The click of the receiver made her close her eyes, a sigh shuddering through her. 'Goodbye, James,' she said to the empty room.

It was over just like that. A word. Goodbye, Caroline: it seemed to echo in the air and she clenched her hands. Two years of happiness, bore-

dom, misery and yearning over in a few moments.
James might not know it yet, but it would dawn on
him after a while. She did not want to make a
dramatic break, load him with more guilt, more unhappiness. Let him think she had merely run off
back to the stage. She need never admit she had
seen him with the other woman. It would make it
easier all round.

She heard the door bell and pulled herself together. Jake looked at her with wry amusement as
he walked past her into Maggie's flat.

'Very fetching,' he muttered.

She laughed, looking down at the bright yellow
silk robe which she had borrowed from Maggie's
wardrobe. 'Not my colour, exactly.'

'Oh, I don't know,' he said, leering. 'Suits you.
Especially the style.'

It was low-lapelled, revealing the frivolously daring nature of the black nightie, and she blushed
slightly. 'I'll get changed.'

'I can't stop,' he said. 'Hang on a minute ... I've
had a word with my TV friends and I think I've
fixed that audition.'

'That's marvellous!'

'Just call me Mr Fix-it,' he said modestly.

'When?'

'When can you make it?'

She looked away. 'I'm not doing anything much
at all,' she said.

Jake pushed his hands into the pockets of his
brown velvet cords. 'Any coffee available? I skipped
breakfast.'

'I'll make you some.' She went into the kitchen

and grimaced at the chaos which the morning revealed to her. There would be a lot of work to do
in here. She put the coffee on and got out two cups.
Jake came in, looked at the mess and exclaimed,
'God Almighty!'

She laughed. 'I'll do it later.'

He stripped off his cashmere sweater, the colour
exactly matching the shade of his cords. 'Got a
pinny? These pants cost a fortune and I don't want
them ruined.'

'There's no need for you to do anything!'

'Heard the expression many hands make light
work?'

She laughed. 'Jake, really!'

He looked behind the door, brought out a bright
blue plastic-coated pinny printed with shocking
pink flowers, two entwined hearts and the romantic
message Hello, Sailor.

Jake looked at it with repulsion. 'It's not me!' he
said, but slipped it over his head.

It made her laugh and he slapped her across her
bottom. 'No taking the mickey—I'm here to work.'
He began to pile the china up methodically and she
continued to make the coffee. When it was ready she
poured two cups and he dried his wet hands. He had
done a large share of the washing up now.

They sat down and drank their coffee, talking
about the TV play. He explained the theme to her.
'The part you audition for is a cameo, but it could
do you a lot of good. Just being seen on the box
helps.'

She asked him a series of eager questions and
listened with absorption as he answered them, his

elbows on the table, his head propped between his hands. It had always been their favourite occupation, shop talk. It had never palled.

He glanced at his watch. 'God, I'm running late!'

'I'm sorry,' she said. 'My fault. I shouldn't have kept you.'

'What are friends for?'

'Borrowing money from, you used to say.'

'And sleeping with,' he added, giving her a sly, wicked look.

Caroline laughed and he said, 'Not that you ever showed me that much friendship, hint though I might.'

'You didn't,' she said firmly.

'No?' He lifted a strongly shaped brow. 'Sure?'

There was a ring at the front door, peremptory and sharp. 'Maggie,' he said. 'I'll let her in as I leave.'

He went out and she grinned, realising he had forgotten to take off Maggie's appalling pinny. She heard the front door open and then the savage note of James's most icy voice. Colour left her face. She jumped to her feet and hurriedly opened the kitchen door.

James looked past Jake at her. Slowly the grey eyes took in every detail of the way she looked, and she saw herself through his eyes and blenched. She was dishevelled and revealingly dressed; the yellow silk robe half open, showing her white throat and the beginning of her breasts, the daring nature of her black nightie. Her feet were bare, as if she had just got out of bed, her light red-gold hair in tumbled disarray. Under James's bitter stare the scarlet colour flooded up her face and throat.

James's features hardened as he took in what she was wearing. He slowly glanced at Jake, who was watching him with a peculiarly bland expression, his lips faintly smiling.

Caroline could find nothing to say to him. She waited for him to speak, instead, her chin lifted defiantly.

James ran those icy eyes over Jake's shirt-sleeved figure, flicking over the gaudy pinny with contempt.

'Get dressed,' he said through tight lips. 'I'm taking you home.'

'No, chum,' Jake drawled, smiling widely now. 'She stays.'

James hit him. It happened too fast for Caroline to take in ... one moment the two men had been looking at each other like savage dogs, the next Jake was flying back across the room and landing with a thud, his head against the wall.

She ran over to him and knelt beside him, aghast. 'Jake, are you all right? Are you hurt?'

He fingered the back of his head, groaning. 'Of course I'm hurt,' he muttered. 'Bone-headed I may be, but if my head hits a wall at speed it damned well hurts!'

She looked round at James. 'There was no need for that,' she said furiously.

James seemed lost for words. He was white and breathing harshly. His hands clenched and unclenched at his sides. The hard-boned face was taut with rage.

'You adulterous little bitch,' he said, breathing hoarsely, then he turned and walked out, slamming the door behind him.

Only then did it dawn on her what he had

thought. She had been so blinded by her own knowledge of his love for another woman that it had not occurred to her that James might suspect her own fidelity. She could have laughed if she had retained any vestige of humour. Instead she swore under her breath, and Jake made a snorting sound.

'Not very ladylike,' he reproved.

She looked down at him. 'Oh, Jake, I'm sorry he did that. I'm afraid he suspected ...'

'Yes, he did, didn't he?' Jake observed with satisfaction.

'Jake,' she said, shaking her head, 'it isn't funny.'

'But he's gone,' Jake pointed. 'And you're still here, It's over, isn't it, Caro?' His eyes delved into her own. 'Finished for good?'

A sigh wrenched at her. 'Yes,' she admitted. James had been angry with her, but she did not fool herself into imagining that he had been jealous or hurt. From what she had seen and heard she could imagine that he had been behaving with circumspect rightness, never making love to the other woman, keeping a careful distance. That would sting now. While he had been keeping what he saw as the rules he would now think she had just gone off and slept with another man without question.

'Don't look so sad,' Jake muttered. 'He isn't worth it. Flinty character, isn't he? When I opened the door he looked me up and down as though I were a caterpillar in his salad.'

'Your pinny, probably,' she observed vaguely.

Jake looked at it with a shout of amusement. 'God, I must look a sight! That explains it.'

He scrambled to his feet and discarded it. 'I must run,' he said, putting on his sweater. 'I'll ring you.'

When he had gone Caroline went into the bathroom and stripped. She ran the bath and showered it with fragrant essences selected from Maggie's generously endowed bathroom cupboard. Sinking into the warm, scented water, she inhaled the delicious steam. Her face had a grim set to it. What was she to do now? After what James thought he had discovered, he might plan to cite Jake as a co-respondent in the divorce case, and she had to stop that. Divorce was easier these days. They could easily get one without any unpleasant public scandals, and the press would certainly seize on anything to do with Jake. James had to be persuaded to see that. He couldn't harm Jake's career with unfounded accusations.

A tear was trickling down her face. It ran into her mouth, salty and unexpected. She hadn't even known she was crying. She rubbed a hand across her eyes, sniffing like a child.

'Oh, James,' she whispered, dropping her face into her wet hands. Where had their love gone? How could the sweet, close warmth of the early days of their marriage turn into the icy severities of recent months?

When had he stopped loving her and begun to love Linda Blare? She ran her fingers into her damp hair, gritting her teeth. She had to make herself believe it: James loved another woman. No matter how much that wounded, she had to face it. It wasn't his fault.

Wasn't it? She began to grow hot and angry, jealousy like acid in her stomach. She thought of the distance there had been between them for months, the coldness he had shown her, the times he had spoken to her as though she were a stupid child. Wasn't any of it his fault? Was she the only one to blame?

CHAPTER THREE

'THERE are practical questions to settle,' Maggie said later. 'You'll have to see him sooner or later.'

Caroline had given her an expurgated version of James's visit and Maggie had listened with calm satisfaction. Now she looked at Maggie and said, half angrily, 'Both you and Jake seem pleased that my marriage has broken up.'

Maggie did not deny it. 'He was too possessive,' she said, her lips firm. 'He kept all your friends away from you. A normal husband expects to share his wife at least a little.'

'My world was so removed from his,' said Caroline, sighing.

'Maybe, but that didn't excuse the ruthless way he detached you from us.' Maggie looked at her with grim humour. 'Now it's going to rebound on his own head.'

'James will be better off without me,' Caroline said flatly, looking down at her own linked hands.

'Hold that thought,' Maggie said wryly. 'He may make trouble yet.'

'No.' Caroline shook her head. 'He'll want a divorce.'

'Don't be too sure. I know lawyers—they hate getting tangled with the law. It's a professional disease.'

It was true, Caroline knew that. James always said that lawyers avoid the processes of the law as they would the plague, knowing too much about the delays and anxieties of it.

'What about your clothes, etc? You'll have to fetch them.'

'I'll go down to the house while he's at court,' said Caroline.

Maggie eyed her. 'Caro, I hate to say this, but you've got to see him. It would be best if it was all done on an amicable level, and you won't achieve that by skulking and avoiding him.'

'I suppose you're right,' Caroline shrugged. 'Anyway, I can fix all that through his solicitor ... knowing James it would be best to do it as much by the book as possible. Proper channels, he would call them.'

'How did you stand the stuffy swine?' Maggie made a face, her black curls shivering around her head. 'He would have driven me insane inside a week.'

'I loved him,' Caroline said simply.

Maggie eyed her, a faint irritation in her glance. 'You're such a simpleton, Caro. You always were—blind as a bat in some directions. Why do you think your stiff-necked James fell for you?'

'I can't imagine,' said Caroline, her mouth turning down at the edges. 'I could never imagine ... we had nothing in common.'

Maggie's eyes rolled upward in disbelief. 'Look in

a mirror some time, girl ... you're a knock-out!
Don't tell me you didn't know?'

Caroline blushed. 'I'm hardly that!'

'God give me patience! Caro, you're too modest.'
Maggie got up and pushed her into the bedroom,
stood her in front of the mirror. 'Look at yourself!'

Caroline looked and saw a girl with light, feathery
red-gold curls arranged around an oval face, the skin
creamy and smooth, the features delicately propor-
tioned. Almond-shaped green eyes, their long black
lashes sweeping to her high cheekbones, stared back
at her in startled surmise. 'My mouth is too wide,'
she pointed out.

'And very passionate,' Maggie retorted. 'Men
think so, I've heard them say so.'

'Men?' Caroline looked at her blankly.

'Jake.' Maggie watched her, eyes veiled.

'Oh, Jake,' Caroline dismissed, smiling easily.

'Yes,' Maggie said below her breath, 'Jake.'

Caroline returned her attention to the mirror.
'My hips are too wide for my bust.'

'Your figure is as sexy as hell,' Maggie retorted
irritably. 'And I quote.'

'Jake again?' Caroline teased.

'Among others ... at the party the comments flew
like rain.'

Caroline flushed. 'Did they indeed?'

'What's the matter with you? Do you prefer to
see yourself as a shrinking violet? You used to be
alive enough. Ask yourself this; if it wasn't your
brilliant mind James fell for, what was it?'

Caroline knew the answer to that, but it had been
so long since he had shown her and she felt her

breath coming fast and hard at the memory. Her eyes grew distant, forgetting Maggie. Her hands went to her breasts, slid from them down her curved body, a blind look on her face.

Maggie watched, frowning. 'If it takes a box of dynamite, I'll wake you up again,' she said with a grim look.

Caroline came back to her presence with a start. 'You're being very kind to me, Maggie. I'm very grateful.'

'What are friends for?' Maggie asked, as Jake had. 'Remember what they used to call us at drama school?'

'The Three Musketeers,' Caroline murmured, laughing.

'You, me and Jake ... the three of us. We swore we'd stick together, get each other parts if we could, share digs and any cash available ... do you remember those plans we used to make?'

'Vividly.'

'Well, for the record, my spare room is yours for as long as you want it, and no strings.' Maggie gave her an impish look. 'Except that you make yourself invisible if I entertain a friend.'

Caroline gave her an amused look. 'Anyone in particular?'

'You'll meet him,' smiled Maggie. 'He's away at the moment, but he'll be back next week.'

'In the profession?'

'Designs sets,' said Maggie. 'He's working in Paris for a month. If you don't like him keep it to yourself.'

'Is it that serious?'

Maggie stretched her arms over her head. 'I think so.'

'For both of you?'

'I'm not sure yet ... about myself, yes, but not about Rob. He plays his cards close to his chest. For all I know he's married with six kids. I have to winkle every piece of information out of him.'

'I hope he's single, then,' Caroline said fervently.

'I'll kill him if he isn't,' said Maggie, and she wasn't joking.

Jake rang that afternoon and arranged for Caroline to audition for the part next day. 'Nervous?' he asked.

'Desperately. I haven't worked for two years, remember.'

'I'll pick you up and take you there. Don't worry, I'll look after you.'

When he had rung off Caroline left the flat and took the train down to her own home. After their marriage it had been James's decision to buy the elegant little house in a Kent village within easy commuting distance of London. It was far enough away from the city to make it possible to have a civilised life there, but near enough for him to be able to get to and from London. At the time it had not dawned on her that he was isolating her from her old circle of friends. By the time she realised it, she was in a state of depression too deep for her to make the break to get out of her misery.

She had made a few friends locally, of course, in the usual way. Housewives she met out shopping, the wife of the local solicitor, the doctor's wife ... James had wanted her to do some local entertaining and for a while they had, but her illness had interrupted all that. It was months since she had seen any of them except briefly by accident.

She let herself into the house. It was as she had known it for months, empty and silent. The smooth, discreet carpeting silenced even her own movements. She looked in at the carefully decorated sitting-room, the furniture spotlessly maintained, the vases of flowers somehow unreal and artificial in that atmosphere.

James had kept her in it like Snow White in her glass casket, airless and lifeless.

She went up the stairs and began to pack. She left most of her clothes; she had only a few things she wanted. Last of all she took the large photograph of James from her bedside table. She looked at the hard, cold handsome face, her fingers trembling Her mouth went dry and she closed her eyes. Then she put it face down on the table and turned to lock the case.

A movement in the door made her start violently. She looked up. 'James!'

He leaned there, a dark, unsmiling figure in his formal clothes, his white shirt startlingly brilliant against the black tie he wore.

'Going somewhere?' he asked, the voice bitingly sardonic.

She looked down at the case and pressed it fumblingly. It refused to lock.

James came forward and his long, thin-fingered hands dealt with it effortlessly. 'Thank you,' she muttered.

He straightened and thrust his hands into his pockets, his shoulders squaring. 'You're moving in with Redway?' He sounded very remote, as though discussing some legal problem with a client.

She flushed deeply. 'No!'

'No?' His dark brows lifted ironically. 'Do you expect me to believe that? After what I saw today?'

'You misunderstood ...' she began, and he broke in with a barbed smile.

'I think not, Caroline. There wasn't much to misunderstand.'

'Jake had just called in,' she said hurriedly. 'It's Maggie's flat. He stopped in to tell me something.'

The grey eyes watched her penetratingly. 'He looked very much at home to me. Does he always visit people in shirtsleeves wearing a vulgar apron?'

Her mouth twitched helplessly at the reference to Maggie's pinny. James saw the movement and his eyes hardened. 'I thought not,' he said coldly. 'I would prefer to be told the truth, Caroline.'

She was suddenly angry. 'Do you always deal in the truth?' She was remembering the woman in his arms and jealousy stabbed inside her.

'What's that supposed to mean?' The brows lifted again, no sign of consciousness in his face.

She looked away. 'Nothing.'

'Do we have to discuss this standing here?' He sounded very calm and controlled and she was relieved because they had to talk, she supposed, and it would be easier to talk if they were both calm.

She followed him into their sitting-room and they sat down in chairs facing each other, like strangers, but then for months past they had shared this house like strangers, so that was nothing new and she should be used to it; but she knew she was not, it hurt like hell.

'What is it you want, Caroline?' he asked, putting

the fingertips of his long hands together as if in prayer and contemplating them with that mask of a face.

'A divorce.' She said the word quickly. It had to be said and only an act of courage could get it out.

He got up and walked away, pushing his hands into his pockets, his back to her. She watched the tall, lean figure with the thick black hair almost brushing the stiff whiteness of his shirt collar. Occasional gleams of silver showed in the strands as he moved. His hair was slowly turning grey and no doubt he would look very distinguished with those silver streaks among the lustrous black.

'And then?' he asked, turned away from her, and his voice sounded unfamiliar.

Caroline was not sure what he meant. Hesitantly she said, 'Then ... then we'll both be free.'

He laughed and the sound shattered her mood of calm. She flinched at the sound of that laughter. He turned and his eyes were no longer cool and controlled. There was rage in them, silvery and fierce.

'Is he a good lover?'

The question made her skin blush hotly. She threw back the rage as if by mirror. 'I told you!'

'You lied,' he said through his teeth. 'I only had to look at you. It may be six months since you were in my bed, but do you think I've forgotten what you look like after love?'

The words made her tremble, her face stricken. She got up to walk out and he took three strides, his body taut. His hands fell on her shoulders, gripping tightly.

'Did he satisfy you? Or should I give him a list of your preferences in bed?'

'You swine!' she hissed, and she had not spoken to him like that before in their relationship, her face alive with hatred, her eyes wild.

'What's the matter? Am I being too frank for you? Did you want your adultery wrapped up in pretty pink ribbons and made respectable by silence?'

'Jake isn't my lover!'

'Do you take me for a fool? He at least didn't try to hide what had happened. He made damned sure I'd know with every look he gave you.' James's face contorted savagely, his jaw held in a vice. 'Not that I needed that confirmation. I guessed from the moment you rang and said you'd spent the night with an old friend ... who else could it have been?'

Caroline stared at him, eyes wide in her flushed face. 'But you've never even met Jake before. He was in the States when we got married.'

'Or you'd never have married me,' he supplied tightly. 'Do you think I've forgotten that telegram he sent us?'

'It was a joke!'

'My God!' He was shaking her shoulders, his fingers hurting. 'Don't lie to me, Caroline. Redway meant every word of it. Every time you've mentioned his name in the past you've given that fact away.'

She was incredulous. She looked at him in dazed disbelief. 'I've hardly ever mentioned him to you!'

'No? You don't even know when you're doing it,' he ground out. 'I got sick of counting the times I heard you say ... Jake did this, Jake said that ... he was never out of your mind.'

'He was never in it!'

'You may have fooled yourself, you didn't fool me.' He looked down at her, his eyes savage. 'One night you talked about him in your sleep.'

She was taken aback. 'I did?'

'You did,' he said grimly.

She lowered her lashes, trying to think. 'What did I say?'

He put a hand under her chin and forced her head up, staring into her eyes. 'I want to see you when I talk to you,' he said. She could remember him once saying that in court he watched the witnesses' eyes and could tell when they were lying. She met his stare directly, openly.

'What did I say in my sleep?'

'His name,' he said, his voice harsh. 'Several times. I woke you up and you looked at me, half doped, and fell back to sleep. After that you didn't talk any more.'

'Was it a nightmare?' She was puzzled, frowning. 'Why did you wake me?'

His lips curled back from his straight white teeth in a hard sneer. 'Do you think I was lying next to my wife listening to her dreaming of another man?'

She tried to pull her chin out of his hand and he slid his fingers round to the back of her head, holding her immobile. 'Stand still!'

'You're hurting!'

'Stand still, then.'

She stood still and he asked, 'How are you planning to support yourself if you're leaving me? Is Redway going to do that?'

'No,' she said sharply. 'I'm going to work.'

'At what?' His voice was ironic.

'Acting ... what else?'

'What else?' he echoed sarcastically. 'It's an over-crowded profession, they say. What makes you think you'll get work?'

'I'm having an audition for a TV part tomorrow!' Her tone was triumphant, but his glance stung.

'Who fixed that, I wonder? Or could I guess?'

Caroline looked away, biting her lip. 'Jake is my friend,' she said, and James laughed again, the sound cruel.

'A polite way of describing it!'

'What do you want me to say?' Her temper ran out of her control, her voice husky and shaking. 'That I'm crazy about him? That I slept with him last night and I'll sleep with him again tonight and tomorrow and every night after it?' The words fell out of her in a fierce torrent, their sound too emotional in this quiet, silken room, out of place, wrong, jarring. 'If that's what you want, James ... very well: Jake's my lover, I want him, I'm divorcing you and going to him.'

His face was like carved stone, his eyes hard and bitter as he watched her mouth spilling out the angry words. Suddenly his hand tightened round her head, he jerked her body towards him with one hand in the small of her back, and his mouth savaged her relentlessly, prying her lips apart, grinding his teeth against her inner mouth. She tried to drag her head back, but he was far too strong for her. His hand clamped her in position, held her head so close that she could not wrench it from beneath his consuming mouth.

She moaned at the pain he was inflicting on her. His teeth were biting into her lips, his fingers wound into her hair, pulling it back to tilt her head.

She struggled so violently that their bodies swayed and crashed to the floor, winding them both. For a dazed moment they lay there, breathing hard. Then Caroline pulled herself together and began to get up, but James swivelled and caught at her with such force that her neckline ripped in his hands. Angrily she looked down at the torn material, then glared at him, her breath catching as she saw his face. He was staring at the white skin laid bare by the ripped neckline. His hand moved heavily, slowly, and fell on her breast.

She tried to speak, but her voice seemed to have dried up. Her heart was thudding below her breast-bone and she felt suddenly sick.

James's eyes flicked to her face and she trem-blingly shook her head in silent protest, her hands pushing his away.

'Yes,' he said in a strange, thickened voice, as if she had spoken.

The long, hard fingers closed around her breast. His dark head came down to it and she groaned. 'No, James!' She could not bear the thought of submit-ting to him with this terrible gulf between them. She thought bitterly of the other woman. It was not herself James wanted—he was merely using her, and that flayed her, it tortured.

Jealously she said: 'Find another woman, James. I don't want you.'

He gave her one look, his face wearing a hard, glazed remoteness which was terrifying in itself. 'You bitch,' he muttered, teeth tight. His hands circled her throat and her eyes darkened as they hardened into iron bands. She gasped, trying to pull his hands down, and his mouth came down on her parted lips, exploring her mouth hotly, beginning a slow, sensual arousal which tore through her defences.

It was months since he had made love to her, and she wanted him. She knew it, aching with the slow-burning fire within her body. Self-respect made her resist with all her strength, though; she struggled, sobbing, using teeth and nails in an attempt to hold him off, and he drew a harsh breath, forcing her back to the floor, the powerful hands violent.

'I mean to have you,' he bit out close to her ear.

'No,' she whispered, her voice faint, her breathing ragged.

He knew exactly what he was doing, how to wring a response from her, even though she was fighting him. He kissed her again, the compelling hands stroking her breasts, curving over her waist and hips, his fingers sensitively teasing her. She kept shaking her head, denying him, but sexual excitement had already betrayed her to him, her breasts were swelling into his hands, her nipples hardening, darkening. His hands slid to her thighs and her body arched in violent, appalling response, a reflex action to which her mind had no defence. 'Caro,' he groaned into her mouth, and his body drove into her while she silently shrieked a bitter protest. Abruptly, as though that lifted her above what was happening, she went cold and stiff. He seemed unaware of it, moving on her urgently, a sharp pleasure in the sound he made, and she heard him with angry hostility. He was using her body against her will, and she felt like an object. She hated him.

When he lay beside her again, breathing hard, she got up and walked out. In her room she showered and dressed again in clean clothes, then turned to go. He stood in the door, face chalk white. She looked at him and saw him flinch as though she had struck him.

'Our marriage was a monumental mistake,' she said. 'We were never suited. You didn't even want children. All I want now is to forget you ever existed.'

James took his hand off her arm and thrust it into his pocket. 'Very well. My solicitor will be in touch with yours if you send me the name.'

'I'll send the name to him,' she said tightly.

As she turned away he said quickly, 'I'll give you an allowance. I don't want you living in penury while you wait for a job.'

'No,' she said sharply. 'I don't want a penny from you.' Then, deliberately, 'Jake will look after me.'

There was a silence in which she walked out and down the stairs. As the door closed behind her she felt as though she could hear some strange, wild echo inside herself, as though the house were a shell full of the sound of the past and her mind had caught that distant murmur, the husky, emotional cry of James's voice long ago as he made love to her. 'Caro,' he had sometimes cried out on the peak of an overmastering pleasure. 'Oh, God, Caro!'

How had that love drained away in the sand of everyday life? Could they have held it if they had tried harder? Was it her fault? Or his? Or both? Had they both contributed to the decay and death of love? She sat in the train like a white statue and thought of her unborn baby with bitter longing. She had wanted that child so much, part of James, part of herself, a life born of their lives, a child for her to

love and hold and care for. James had not wanted
it and although he had been kind to her when she
lost it he had never said he was sad about her loss.
That had divided them these past six months, and
she had thought he could do nothing which could
hurt her more.

She had been wildly wrong. He had fallen in love
with another woman, and maybe the separation between them this past six months had helped to feed
his attraction for Linda Blare, so that might be her
fault. She no longer knew or cared.

Because today he had finally killed her love. The
brutal passion he had shown her had been so love-
less, so barbaric, that she could only think of him
with fear and contempt.

CHAPTER FOUR

In the privacy of the bathroom next morning Caroline saw the marks James had left on her body, and
anger rose inside her, although the anger was more
caused by the mental bruises he had left rather
than the physical ones which other people might
see. Naked, she stood in front of the floor-length
mirror and touched the dark mark of his fingers on
her breast. How could he have done such a thing?
On her shoulders lay several tiny red stains, like

faint burn marks, but it was the bruises his enforc-
ing hands had made which caught the eye. They
stood out on her arms, her shoulders, her breasts,
and she knew she would have to wear something all-
concealing to hide them from Maggie. It would be
degrading for anyone to know what James had done
to her. She felt like the victim of rape, and although
he was her husband wasn't that what he had done
to her?

He had used her; it was that which stung. Had
there been any deep personal passion driving him
she could have forgiven it, but it had been temper,
sheer temper which caused his behaviour.

She had been his possession. She had, he thought,
given herself to another man, and James could not
forgive that. He had taken her to stamp his own
brand on her, as though she were a straying animal.

Her eyes flashed as she turned away. The sooner
she arranged the divorce the better.

Jake looked her up and down with wry comment
when he arrived to take her for the audition. 'You
can't wear that,' he said flatly.

'Why not?'

'Paddy will want to see something of you,' he said,
mouth quirking insolently.

Caroline flushed. The high-necked sweater and
jeans she was wearing had seemed ideally suitable
and they concealed what she wanted concealed.

'I'm an actress, not a strip tease artist!'

'Don't be po-faced, darling,' said Jake, shaking his
head.

'I warned you,' Maggie said, and it was true, she
had.

Jake glanced at his watch. 'Well,' he shrugged,

making a face, 'it will have to do. We're running late. Paddy won't wait for you.'

In the car she apologised and he took a hand off the wheel to pat hers briefly. 'Okay, sweetie, forget it. Paddy can always ask you to strip.' And his quick, teasing grin assured her that that was a joke, but she wondered if it was, in fact.

She was nervous. It was a long time since she had done any acting and she knew perfectly well that she had only got this audition to please Jake. She knew how things worked. They would see her, to placate him, and then they would quietly get someone else, someone with more talent and more experience.

But when she met the director he stared at her face intently, eyes narrowed, got her to walk around the studio floor while the other men with him watched. She had to hold her head up yet avoid tripping over the cables which trailed everywhere, and it was an ordeal. She felt like Daniel in the lions' den.

'How does she shape?' the director shouted, apparently to nobody, and a disembodied voice replied. Caroline heard the buzzing but could see nobody until she looked up and saw faces at a glass box window, then she looked hopelessly at Jake, who was eyeing one of the girls who walked around the place, long-legged as giraffes, their faces haughty, like models. The girl looked at Jake, knowing he was watching her, and he winked. She switched on a smile like a lighthouse beam, but Jake did not follow up.

The men talked about Caroline as if she were not there and they asked her to do nothing she knew as acting. They were merely interested in her as a functioning face, she gathered. Did she look good on the screen, it seemed to boil down to, and she wondered if she had been mad coming along here, asking for humiliation.

'Okay,' said Paddy, sharply, as though a decision had been made, although she had not followed their talk. 'Let's hear her, then.'

She looked at Jake. He stepped over a cable and took her arm. 'Got your words ready?'

'What shall I do?'

He glanced at Paddy, who unrolled a script from one of his capacious pockets and threw it to Jake. 'God,' said Jake, looking at it, then grinned. 'Something else he's doing. High culture stuff.' Over his shoulder Caroline read a page and sighed.

'I'll do it with her,' Jake said to Paddy.

Paddy lifted one eyebrow. 'If you say so.'

Caroline saw all the men exchange knowing looks. They took her for Jake's latest woman, imagined he was pushing her because he wanted to please her. They would not expect anything of this test.

She thought of James using her ruthlessly last night, of Jake and Maggie so sure they knew best what she should do with her life, and her temper flared to boiling point. She was sick of being pushed around, of being patronised.

They ran through the few pages Jake had chosen to do with her and she let him direct her, pressing an interpretation on her, but when they did the scene for real in front of the camera she bit the words out as if she bit off heads, her voice sharp and clear, her face edged.

Jake looked at her in astonishment. It was not the way he had told her to do the part, and he shrugged his broad shoulders.

Paddy watched, head on one side, stuck an unlit cigar in his mouth and rubbed a line of fingers along one palm, rolling the cigar around thoughtfully.

When they had finished he came over and turned her head with his broad, blunt-fingered hand, as if she were a plastic doll.

'Hmm,' he said thoughtfully. 'Come over to my office, both of you.'

In the tiny, metallic blue office he sat in his swivel chair and stuck his feet on the desk, crumpling up a letter which lay on the desk and chucking it into the waste-paper basket. 'Tell me about your career, Caro.'

Jake began to talk and Paddy waved a finger at him. 'I said the girl.'

Caroline curtly told him the few details which were all she could offer. 'Then you married?'

'Yes.'

'Marriage a wash-out?'

The brutality of the question went home like a stab. 'Yes,' she said, parting her lips slightly.

'Tough.' It didn't interest him, all that interested him was her commitment. 'It isn't a big part,' he pointed out. 'Walk in, walk out, few lines ... a lot of costume changes.'

She nodded.

'Well,' he said, getting up, 'we'll let you know.'

Jake was whistling as they drove back to her flat. 'That went better than I'd feared,' he said.

'Glad you're pleased.'

He looked at her. 'What's up with you? You've

been like a bear with a sore head all day.'

'Nothing,' she said, lying.

He followed her into Maggie's flat. 'Come on, give, Caro. I'm your buddy, remember?'

'A headache,' she said. 'That's all.'

'Don't go all feminine and devious on me, will you?' he asked, watching her. 'What I always liked about you was your directness.'

She relaxed, smiling at him. She was being unfair to him. He had done his best for her, and any patronage had been on the part of his friends, not on his side. She should be grateful, not resentful.

'I'm sorry,' she said.

'You're going through a bad patch,' he told her soothingly. 'It will get better.'

Will it? she asked herself. Will I ever get over James? Marriage involved a great deal of commitment, a great deal of give and take, and all those little moments which pass day after day, adding to the store of memories, kept coming back and sticking in her mind like burrs in a dog's coat. She couldn't shake them off. She was angry with James at the moment, but anger couldn't last for ever, and her body still held him like an illness, a germ in the blood.

Jake took her out to lunch to cheer her up. He chose a fashionable eating place, the sort of restaurant it did an actor good to be seen at, and he seemed to know everybody, or be known. Their arrival caused a stir. Faces turned, voices dropped, whispering, and Caroline knew from the glances she was getting that people were asking: 'So who's that with Jake Redway? What's going on there?' Jake was unperturbed by it. He expected it, he quite liked it.

He grinned at her rakishly as they sat down.

'You're looking very sexy.' She had changed at his request, the sweater and jeans discarded, and she wore one of the outfits she had bought the other day, a high-necked, long-sleeved white silk dress. It was timeless and simple and it fitted like another skin. The sleeves were filmy, almost transparent, but she didn't think they revealed the bruises James had left. From the high roll collar a slit ran, widening, to the cleft of her breasts, giving the formality an exciting sexiness.

They ordered at their leisure. Jake was, it seemed, in no hurry. He put a hand across the table and took hold of one of hers, held it as he talked, lightly. He reminisced about their drama school days and she was surprised by how much he remembered. His recall was almost perfect.

'You seem nostalgic,' she commented.

'I enjoyed it all,' he said. 'Didn't you?'

'Yes, of course!' It had been a memorable period of her life, but she had not retained every moment of it intact, as Jake had obviously done, and he surprised her, because he had played around so much, full of schoolboy jokes and wild behaviour.

'You know what they say,' he murmured. 'To travel hopefully is better than to arrive! I wanted badly to be a success, but looking forward to the idea was more exciting than getting it.'

'That's sad,' she said, looking across the table at him in a worried fashion. 'Jake, I thought you loved acting.'

'I do,' he assured her. 'I love the job itself. It's all the things that go with it that bothers me. I've reached a high level too quickly. Too many outside

things keep getting in between me and my work ...
oh, it's hard to explain ... you would have to be in
that position to understand; parties, publicity, important people to chat up ... and all the time it's
the job that matters, but I have to fight to work
these days. People are always trying to stop me, get
me to do something else.'

She listened, her face sober. 'You must be firm.
Put your foot down.'

He grimaced. 'I try, but it's true; the money
people matter a hell of a lot. They have to be kept
sweet and they expect me to dance attendance on
them if I want their money for films or plays. Our
real life is inside the theatre, yet it stretches out in
all directions. I have to be on show almost twenty-
four hours a day, and that's damned tiring.'

'Poor Jake,' she said, softly, holding out her hand,
and he took it, lifting it to his mouth, brushing his
lips lightly over the back.

'It's wonderful to have you back,' he said, looking
into her eyes with a serious expression. 'I've missed
you like hell.'

Someone walked past their table at that moment
and a peculiar frisson ran along Caroline's spine, as
though a cold finger had touched her. She flicked
her gaze past Jake's shoulder and saw a long, lean
back. Her heart stopped and started again, faster.
She looked back at Jake, very casually, and smiled at
him.

'I've missed you,' she said, a sigh ending the
words.

'Why make it sound so grim?' Jake was teasing
her. 'You and Maggie were the best friends I ever
had, real friends, ones I could trust. The only people

I ever knew who didn't want something.'

She frowned. 'You're very cynical, Jake.'

'I've learnt to be,' he shrugged, mouth turning down. 'There's always a string attached, Caro, always a pay-off some time along the line.'

Her eyes widened, her lashes swept down to cover them. After a pause she said quietly, 'Is there for me, Jake?' and looked up quickly at his face.

Faint red swept up his features. 'No,' he said, far too quickly, and she was left staring at him in wary appraisal. 'No,' he said again, in a strong, half-angry way. 'I got you that audition for my own reasons. I want you back in the theatre, where you belong. Maggie and I both want you back—Caro, you're only half alive.' He leaned forward, speaking urgently. 'We both remember you as the brightest of the trio, you were warm and sweet and very alive. Your marriage has dimmed you. You have to come back where you belong.' He clasped her hand tighter. 'So, no pay-off, darling. No strings. I wouldn't do that to you.' His eyes were serious. 'You mean too much to me.'

'Do I?' She watched him, still frowning, trying to unravel his motives.

He shrugged his broad shoulders. 'Whatever I feel about my work is wrapped up with how I feel about you and Maggie ... the tough times we had when we were young, the budgeting and cheap food, the dreaming and planning for the future ... it was a heady time for all of us, and nothing since has meant as much.'

It was true. Even her life with James had been haunted by the bright shadow of those days with Jake and Maggie, she had never shaken it off, and maybe that had contributed to the ruin of her marriage.

She looked past his shoulder and James was watching them from a table further down the restaurant. His eyes were sombre, his face a cold mask. She tightened inside, meeting his stare for a second before flicking her eyes past him as though he were a stranger, letting them move over other faces with the same distant expression before returning her gaze to Jake.

'We had too many dreams then,' she said sadly. 'Life is a little tasteless when you come out of your dreams, isn't it?'

He leaned forward eagerly. 'Is that how you found it?'

She mentally drew back, struck by the look in his eyes, but with James watching them she let Jake hold her hand and smiled at him. 'That's how I found it,' she agreed, and it was true, and she wondered if both she and Jake had found reality less exciting than dreams.

Glancing vaguely upwards a few moments later she found she could see James in a gilt-framed mirror hanging on the wall above their table. He was drinking, leaning back in his chair, his eyes on their table. There was nobody else at his table and he had no meal in front of him, so she assumed he was waiting for his companion to show up, and wondered if she would see Linda Blare at any moment.

Deliberately she let her eyes drift towards him and saw his hand shake. The glass hit the table as he put it down, spilling wine in a golden fountain. He dabbed at it with his napkin, head bent, and she saw colour run along his hard cheekbones.

It elated her to have this effect on him. He had been impervious for so many months, a cold, distant companion. Now she was aware of having the power to prick that arrogant ego of his, and she was enjoying exerting that power. She could guess why he was so disturbed by her presence. James had a strong sense of morality, of what should and should not be done, and no doubt he had shocked himself by the violence with which he had forced her yesterday. She was a permanent reminder to him of his loss of control. She was embarrassing him.

She was fiercely glad at the thought. She wanted to hurt him—he had hurt her again and again for months, and last night had been the nadir of their relationship. She felt as if she had somehow risen from it, a phoenix from the ashes of their marriage, strengthened by the very pain he had inflicted on her.

Someone paused at their table and Jake reluctantly took his eyes from Caroline to glance around. 'Hi. Simone,' he said, smiling.

Caroline looked up, too, and recognised her immediately, with the little shock it does give to see a really famous face in real life.

'Jake, how are you?' Simone Corona was very tall, blonde, elegantly dressed, and had a clever, cynical face which was yet oddly beautiful, her features rakishly sharp, more masculine than feminine, yet pulling the eye to admire.

She flicked her cold blue eyes towards Caroline, summed her up with a look and conferred a brief, polite smile, like an accolade. Even her most fleeting expressions were familiar from her films, and Caroline could read this one; a look meant to express dry appreciation for her looks and cynical understanding of her presence with Jake. She found herself smiling back, eyes twinkling, and Simone gave her another quick look.

'Sim, I'd like you to meet Caro,' said Jake, giving the other woman a strange look.

'Caro?' Simone repeated the name, staring at her. Then she looked at Jake. 'Caro?'

Jake's face was blank. 'Yes,' he said.

Turning, the other woman held out a hand. 'Hallo, Caro,' she said, examining her face more closely, her eyes narrowed. 'I've heard about you, but I never expected to meet you.'

Caroline was puzzled, amused. She lifted her light red-gold head with a wary smile, met the long, probing stare. 'And I certainly never expected to meet you, Miss Corona.' Her eyes were wide and bright. 'I'm a great admirer of yours, as Jake may have told you. I've learnt a lot about pacing and control from your work. You make it look so easy when we all know it's very hard work.'

Simone's wide, strong mouth deepened with a genuine smile. 'Jake did mention that he used to take you to see my films.'

'Six or seven times each, I seem to remember,' Jake put in, grinning. 'Caro cannibalised you, Sim —ate you up and lived on it for weeks. I used to tease her when I saw your style coming out in her work at the school ... ah-ha, I used to say, a touch of the Coronas.'

Caroline blushed and laughed. 'I grew out of being so obvious,' she said quickly.

Simone's eyes were amused, openly pleased. 'We all learn on each other,' she soothed. She glanced

down the restaurant. 'I've a date with a very tough
opponent, so I must go ... I'm late already, and nobody keeps the great man waiting! Jake, I'm having
a party on Saturday. Come and bring Caro, then I
can talk to her without interruption.' She glanced at
Caroline again, blue eyes friendly. 'I've heard so
much about you from Jake I feel I know you
already, please come.'

'We'll be there,' Jake promised, and Caroline
smiled her thanks.

She watched as Simone walked away and then her
heart turned over as she saw at whose table she was
stopping. Jake was talking lightly, 'She's just as she
appears on screen ...' His words faded out of her
mind and she couldn't take her eyes off James's face.
He was greeting Simone, bending his tall figure. As
Simone sat down James glanced down the restaurant
and quickly Caroline looked away. Why was Simone
Corona having lunch with him?

Jake took her back to Maggie's flat an hour later
and left her with a quick kiss on the cheek. Maggie
was curled up in a chair, crocheting a circular
cushion, groaning over it.

'This will be mud-coloured by the time I've
finished it! I've unpicked it six times, but it still
goes wrong.' She flung it aside with a gesture of
repulsion. 'Now,' she said, grinning at Caroline,
'how did the audition go?'

Caroline told her about it and Maggie grinned,
nodding. 'Jake has pulled every string he's got, I
expect.'

'Unethical,' Caroline said drily.

'But quite usual in our world,' Maggie shrugged.
'After all, it helps to have a reference.'

Caroline met her eyes coolly. 'All those men thought I was Jake's woman.'

Maggie grinned. 'So?'

'I don't like it,' Caroline said firmly. 'I'm not, and I don't want to have people thinking I am.'

'Don't be so stuffy,' said Maggie. 'Didn't we all swear to get each other jobs; wouldn't you do the same for Jake, if you could?'

Caroline looked at her uncertainly.

'Well, wouldn't you? If you could get him a part, wouldn't you try it?'

'Yes,' Caroline admitted, knowing that she would.

'There you are, then . . . don't get so uptight about it. Jake knows what he's doing. He's got me parts in the past, several.'

'Has he?' Caroline brightened.

'Of course! I've even got him one.' Maggie's eyes danced.

'Really? What?'

'Back legs of a horse in panto,' Maggie grinned, and Caroline giggled.

'That was when we were at school! I remember it!' As if it were yesterday, the excitement, the fun, the teasing as Maggie, Jake and herself went off to work for a month in a panto at a northern seaside town. They had shared cut-price digs, with a land-lady who had a permanent cold and served fried eggs for breakfast which were already cold and slipped greasily about on the serving plate. Caroline had been a fairy, she remembered, grinning. The brief white tulle dress had made her look about twelve, Jake said. A sexy twelve, he had added, leer-ing, and kissed her quickly before she hit him with a wet flannel.

Maggie was watching her. 'You didn't need any help getting your part. The director fancied you.'

Caroline flushed. 'He was fifty if he was a day! And bald and fat!'

'He still fancied you, darling,' Maggie said drily. 'Jake wanted to punch his nose, but he was afraid of getting the sack ... we all needed that money.'

'What there was of it,' Caroline said, sighing. It had barely covered the cost of their digs and they had shivered around one ring of a gas fire during the daytime, sharing warmth and food, eating a bag of chips between them after the show each night. 'I'll keep you warm,' Jake had offered, putting an arm round her, and she had leaned on his shoulder and absorbed his body heat gratefully.

'Jake worries me,' she said aloud to Maggie, frowning.

Maggie stared at her with veiled eyes. 'Why?' Her voice sounded odd.

'He isn't enjoying his success, is he?'

'Isn't he?' Maggie was giving nothing away, but Caroline knew her too well. Maggie wasn't surprised by what she had just said.

'He looks back all the time,' Caroline said soberly. 'Now he's got to the top he isn't sure it was what he wanted.'

'Isn't life always like that? Aren't we all disillusioned and prone to hanker after something we haven't got?' Maggie smiled wryly. 'They used to call it the human condition ... the hankering for an Eden we could barely remember, a dream we'd half forgotten.'

'Yes,' Caroline said, struck. 'That was what went wrong with my marriage, I'm beginning to think ...

I couldn't get over the dreams we shared, you, me and Jake. The life James offered me seemed unsatisfactory after them.'

'You didn't belong,' Maggie said quickly. 'He was too possessive. At your wedding I mentioned Jake to him in passing ... nothing important, just his name, and your husband gave me a look which went right through my shoulder-blades. From then on I was out, and he made sure I knew it. I got the cold shoulder every time he saw me.' She looked at Caroline directly. 'He was jealous of Jake, wasn't he? And I'd shown that I was on Jake's side, so I was out, too. We all were ... he wasn't sharing you with anyone.'

Caroline was shaken. James, jealous? She looked back over their marriage and wondered how she could have been so blind. Of course, it explained everything. James had been jealous of her friendships with Jake and Maggie. He had read an importance in them that she had not been aware of at the time. Now, looking back, she could see that he might not have been without cause. Jake and Maggie had been far more important to her than she had realised under the spell of her passion for James.

The dreams she had shared with them had hung on inside her mind, haunting her like an unforgotten melody. James had said that she had talked of Jake all the time, without even knowing it, and maybe she had. How could she have forgotten him? They had been too close for too long. If Jake had been her brother, James would not have expected anything else, but he had not been prepared to admit another man's importance to her.

'He wouldn't even share you with a child,' Maggie went on, thinking aloud, and Caroline felt the words go right through her like a spear. She stared at Maggie, eyes stretched wide.

'W-what did you say?'

Maggie threw her a look, repeating the words. 'He wanted you to himself,' she said. 'What other reason could there be? He was a very conventional man in other ways, exactly the sort of man to want children. Yet he didn't.'

Caroline felt her skin grow icy, her head throb with agony. Yes, she thought. Why didn't I think of that before? She remembered suggesting that if they had a child she could get a nurse to look after it during the times James was at home. 'Then you wouldn't be disturbed, darling,' she had pleaded. 'If the nursery was at the top of the house you wouldn't hear a sound.' He had refused angrily, coldly, his eyes like rapiers. Jealous, she thought dully. The concept of James's jealousy had never entered her head before. She had seen his behaviour as coldly selfish, based on his view of his own importance. And it was selfish, she thought. But if jealousy lay at the bottom of it ... there would have been something she could have done to reassure him. She could have made him see that her feeling for him would not be diminished by having a child. Couldn't she?

'Thank goodness you've got away from him,' Maggie said. 'I never liked him.'

'No,' said Caroline, staring at her. Maggie's views were biased. James had insulted her. It was easy to dislike someone who first shows dislike to you, and James had made no secret of his coldness towards Maggie. Maggie was a human being, with her own axe to grind, her own feelings. Human beings were like animals in that they had their own small strip of territory to patrol, their own tribe to protect. Maggie's territory was the theatre, Jake and Caroline were her tribe. She saw it very simply.

'You should never have married an outsider,' she said now, her voice complacent. 'But it's over.'

People, Caroline thought, are a problem. Why do they have as many corners as a Chinese puzzle? Why is life so complicated and painful? In an ideal world Maggie and Jake would get on like a house on fire with James, and he with them. Childishly, when she married him, she had expected it to happen like that. She had fallen into love immediately, wildly, and never thought about the consequences, the repercussions.

What a fool I've been, she told herself.

Jake rang her two days later with the news that the audition had been successful. 'The job's yours,' he announced, elated.

'Jake! Are you sure?' She was strung-up, trembling.

'Paddy just told me,' he said. 'There were two other possibles, but he decided to give it to you.'

Because Jake wanted her, she thought wryly, but she knew she would not let that stand in her way. Maggie came over to mouth silently, 'Get it?'

She nodded and Maggie grinned, ear to ear, taking the phone from her and shouting, 'Terrific!' at Jake. She gave the phone back and Jake groaned, 'She's split my eardrums!'

'What can I say? I'm overwhelmed,' Caroline told him.

'Have dinner with me,' he retorted.

'I'd love to,' she said.

'We'll celebrate.'

'And Maggie?' she asked, because that would make the threesome as before, the old team.

'If you like.' He sounded suddenly very dry.

'Can't come,' Maggie bellowed down the receiver, pulling it from her mouth, and Jake said cheerfully, 'Not again! I'll be deaf if she keeps this up!' Then he laughed, his voice light. 'Just us, then, Caroline.'

Alarm bells rang in her head and she looked at Maggie, who was looking bland. 'Right,' she said, but her mind was ticking like an atom bomb.

'I'll pick you up at eight,' he said. 'Wear something stunning—I want to show you off.'

When she had rung off she looked at Maggie, who was ecstatic, as if she had got the part herself. 'How does it feel?' Maggie asked her. 'To be working again?'

'Fabulous,' said Caroline, but she was secretly disturbed, because Jake was expecting something from her, she had known that by his voice, and Maggie was deliberately staying out of it. She had no other date for that evening, Caroline was aware of it. She was leaving them alone and if she was matchmaking she was enjoying it. Her eyes had a vivid sparkle, as though she were triumphant. Maggie and Jake were both aware of something which was now slowly beginning to dawn an Caroline, and she shivered, trying to push away the suspicion which had begun to grow on her little by little during the last few days.

CHAPTER FIVE

MAGGIE insisted that she must buy a new dress. Caroline had a bank account of her own—James had insisted on that—but she had not wanted to draw on it after leaving him. Maggie made a wry face over that statement. 'Why ever not? In my opinion, you've earned every penny of it. If he'd employed a housekeeper, he would have had to pay her. He paid you, instead.'

Caroline shivered. 'I can't look at it like that.'

'Start now,' Maggie advised. 'He's turned you into a dutiful slave, girl. You ran his house for him. You deserved every penny he gave you. He can afford it. He's well off, isn't he?'

Yes, James was wealthy. His father had been a judge and had left him a sound private income when he died. James earned a good income from his work, too. There had never been any shortage of money.

Maggie talked her into it in the end and they went off shopping. It was Maggie's favourite occupation. She adored clothes. She spent two hours that afternoon before she was prepared to be satisfied with the dress they finally chose.

When Caroline was ready Maggie came into the bedroom to stare at her intently. Caroline looked at her questioningly. 'Well? How do I look?'

Maggie's eyes danced. 'Do I need to tell you? Jake will do that, I suspect.'

Caroline gave her a quick, anxious look and said nothing. Her eyes returned to her own reflection. The dress was like nothing she had ever owned before. Ultra-sophisticated, it was black silk, heavy and smooth, clinging to her body where it touched, leaving her white shoulders bare, cupping her breasts in pointed stiff shells of material which seemed to stay up by magic, The bruises James had left had almost gone. Maggie glanced at her arms and frowned, touching one bluish mark with a finger. 'How did you get that?'

Caroline felt herself flush and Maggie looked at her quickly, then growled under her breath. 'Don't tell me, I can guess.'

She couldn't even suspect, Caroline thought, shuddering. No doubt Maggie imagined some struggle, a quarrel ending in blows, but she could not surely conceive the thing James had done. It was too barbaric.

'You need jewellery with it,' Maggie told her.

Caroline had left the jewellery box James had given her on the dressing-table in her elegant, empty home. 'I haven't any,' she said, without a shred of regret for the string of pale, matched pearls she had inherited from James's mother, who had been dead before their wedding, or any of the lovely things James had given her afterwards. They had been toys for a captive, she thought, and they were worthless to her.

'I can lend you some good costume stuff,' said Maggie, diving into her own bedroom. She returned with a large ivory box, worked with elephants in

long lines. 'Rob gave it to me,' she said, showing it
to her, pleasure in her face. She opened it and rum-
aged through the tangled jewellery, making Caroline laugh.

'Here, let me.' She disentangled the necklaces
slowly and with method and Maggie grimaced over
it.

'I know, I'm a sloven.'

'You always were,' Caroline said, affectionately.
Vital, impulsive, always in a rush, Maggie always
had been untidy.

Together they discussed which piece of jewellery
Caroline should wear and decided on a heavy, barbaric silver necklet which Rob had brought Maggie
from Egypt. The rows of wide silver rings were
filled with medallions covered with Arabic signs. It
felt cold and heavy on her bare throat and altered
the whole appearance of the gown.

Caroline studied herself with surprise. Her own
reflection shook her. Slim, her body rounded in
seductive curves under the black silk, her hair
blazed around her face like fire and the silver necklet gave her features a sensuous promise she had
never seen in them before. Her almond-shaped eyes
were a very bright green, her mouth generously
warm.

Maggie whistled under her breath. 'I can't wait to
see Jake's face!'

Again Caroline felt that warning signal in her
head. She gave Maggie a tense glance. 'Maggie ...'

Whatever she had been about to ask was interrupted by the loud ring of the door bell. 'He's here,'
said Maggie, and Caroline wondered if she had
imagined the faint relief in her tones.

Maggie went off to open the door and Caroline followed more slowly, picking up her small black purse and a silver-threaded white shawl which Maggie had lent her for the evening.

Jake was laughing as she came into the room. He turned his head and stopped laughing and his eyes stretched. 'Wow!' he muttered huskily.

Maggie had a smug smile. 'I thought you'd be impressed,' she said. She gave them both an embracing look. 'Enjoy yourselves, you two!'

Maggie was weaving plots, Caroline thought, as Jake drove her away from the flat. What exactly was in her mind as she shoved them into each other's arms so blatantly?

Over dinner in a charming little restaurant, Jake said: 'You haven't forgotten we said we'd go to Simone's party? That's why I wanted you to look stunning. I want you to make an impression. Simone could be very useful to you.'

She frowned, distaste in her green eyes. 'Is that the only reason for being nice to her, Jake?'

He gave her a quick look. 'You know it isn't. I admire her, and I know you do, but you have to remember that it helps to know people. Without talent you would get nowhere, but even with talent you can fall through a hole in the world unless there are people who will help you. A lot of success in our world is being in the right place at the right time ... like catching a train. If you miss it, you may miss out all along the line, however talented you may be.'

'You've changed,' she said flatly. On the surface he had seemed to be the same Jake, but underneath she saw now that he had altered a good deal, toughened, hardened, grown cynical.

'So have you,' he said, his eyes sweeping down over her body in the black silk dress. His glance was acquisitive, she saw that now, and she was disturbed by it. 'You're ravishing,' he told her. 'Sexy and beautiful. You're going to make quite an impact. I've seen the preliminary designs for the Josephine costumes, and some of them will be a knockout on you.'

He began to talk about the TV series and her feelings of alarm and anxiety faded as the old Jake re-surfaced and her pleasure in shop talk took over. They did not hurry their meal, but at a quarter to ten Jake looked at his watch and said with a sigh of regret, 'Time to go along to Simone's party. A pity, I was enjoying our little tête-à-tête.'

Caroline had been enjoying it, too, she had to admit that. When Jake put her in the passenger seat of his car and joined her behind the wheel, she glanced at him through her lashes and felt a little lurch of the heart. He was attractive; he always had been. Why hadn't she ever felt the tug of that attraction before? She had always seen him in that brotherly light. Now she knew the fraternal image was fast fading and Jake intended that it should. He turned his head and gave her a slow, assessing glance.

'Quiet, aren't you? Something worrying you?'

'I'm not sure,' she said frankly, meeting his look.

Jake moved along the seat and turned her chin with one light finger. 'Stop thinking about him,' he said, but his tone was not light, it was sharp, and his eyes were dark.

'I wasn't,' she said, surprised.

'No?' Jake studied her. 'You're with me,' he

said. 'And I like my women to think of me, not somebody else.'

'I'm not one of your women, Jake,' she said sharply.

His finger smoothed down her cheek, caressed the line of her mouth. 'That's right,' he said softly. 'You never have been. You're unique, Caroline, out on your own. I could never confuse you with anyone else.'

'Do you confuse the others?' she asked, frowning.

'Frequently,' he said drily. 'They all get to seem the same in the end. It doesn't matter a damn which one of them I'm with.'

She shivered. 'That's terrible!'

'Isn't it?' He laid his whole hand along her cheek. 'Even with my eyes shut in the dark I think I would know your face.'

Her skin prickled at the tone. 'Hadn't we better go? We'll be very late at the party.'

Jake had closed his eyes. He leant towards her, his face blind, his features carved like marble. His fingers drifted over her skin delicately, as though he were a burglar picking a lock with his eyes shut. Caroline sat, frozen, staring at him. The long fingers touched her eyelids, closing her eyes, and she inhaled sharply. They moved down the delicate lines of her face, travelling along the fine bones.

'Caroline,' he breathed.

She moved breathlessly, her hands flung to his shoulders. 'No, Jake!'

'Yes,' he said huskily. 'I've waited too long already.'

His mouth closed over hers forcibly and she

gasped. He took advantage of the opening of her lips to explore her mouth fully, his hand propelling her head backwards to make it easier. She was dazed by the strangeness of being in his arms like this—he had never touched her with such hunger, such longing, and she could feel it intensely in every pore. Her hands closed over his shoulders. For a few seconds she resisted, then she relaxed involuntarily and, feeling her go limp, Jake pulled her closer, leaning down on her body, his mouth warm and hard and compelling.

She felt his hands move down over her and shuddered in response. She had not wanted him to touch her, yet now she did not want him to stop. The stroking movements of his warm fingers soothed her as though she were a frightened animal, reassured by the physical contact. 'Caro, Caro,' he whispered against her ear.

'We can't,' she muttered huskily.

He laughed very softly. 'Can't? We are ... don't tell me this is one-sided, darling, because I'm not an inexperienced boy.' His lips descended gently to her throat, played over it without haste, caressing it lingeringly. She was swept with sensual pleasure, responding without thought, her neck arched, her body quivering.

Jake lifted his head and she felt him looking at her. Her eyes flew open and she flushed deeply, aware that he knew how he had affected her.

'Can't we?' he asked mockingly. He dropped a brief, hard kiss on her mouth, then straightened and started the car. In the passing light of a street lamp she saw his features, brilliant with satisfaction, and she groaned.

He glanced sideways quickly. 'Guilty?' he asked drily.

'Jake, I'm married!'

'For the present,' he agreed. 'That can be altered.' He gave her a dancing smile. 'You are divorcing him, aren't you, Caroline?'

She didn't answer, but yes, she thought, she had to divorce James. There was no future for them. Their marriage was over.

'He'll find someone else,' Jake said lightly.

'He already has,' she said, then bit the words back, but too late.

'Has he?' Jake turned to stare. 'Well, well ... you didn't tell Maggie that.'

She bitterly regretted having let that slip. 'Please,' she said, 'forget what I said.'

'As you like,' Jake shrugged, but he looked very pleased with himself. He was delighted to hear that James had someone else. He began to whistle under his breath, his smile broad.

When they had parked he helped her out of the car and she looked up at him in secret appraisal. He was a sexy animal, she thought, there was no point in denying that, and she could not imagine how she had remained unaware of his charismatic charm for so long, seeing him only as the brother she had never had. Their old relationship had unsexed him for her, made him safe, defused the time bomb of his physical allure. Now something had altered. She saw him with new eyes and she was disturbed by what she saw.

He turned, putting an arm around her waist, his fingers tightening on her. The lazy, cynical smile touched his mouth. 'Shall we make our entrance?'

Her lashes dropped, hiding her eyes. 'Why not?'

He looked at her hard. 'Caro,' he murmured, and she glanced at him from under her lashes. A mocking look touched his eyes. 'Caro,' he said again, this time teasingly. 'Stop worrying about it ... just let it happen.'

'What?' she asked him with slight hauteur.

'You know what I'm talking about,' he said.

She lifted her lashes and her green eyes shone out at him, cold and hard. 'Is this the pay-off time, Jake?' she asked cuttingly. 'Are you pulling the string, after all?'

He drew a sharp, angry breath. 'No, I'm damned well not,' he snapped. 'I ought to slap you for that!'

'So long as we know where we are,' she said vaguely, turning away. He caught her arm and shook it, frowning down at her.

'We both know,' he said. 'But it has nothing to do with any pay-off, Caro, and don't try to pretend you think it has. I'm insulted you should even suggest it.'

She sighed. 'I'm sorry. But how could I be sure? You said yourself that it was the way things got done.'

'Not between us,' he said harshly. 'Never suggest it again. You mean too much to me for that sort of game.'

Again she felt that strange shiver of warning, her brows jerking together. She lifted her eyes to his face, probing his expression. 'Jake ...' What she had been about to say was never said. His arms came round her in a violent, convulsive moment and he held her against his shoulder, stroking her hair.

'Don't you really know, Caroline?' His voice quivered. He laid his cheek against her hair, rubbing it softly backwards and forwards. 'You're so small, I could put you in my pocket, keep you for my mascot. You were such a little thing, so fine-boned and nervy, all eyes. When you smiled your face lit up and I felt like kissing you, but you never gave me a green light.' He took her face between his hands, tipping it backward, his fingers winding into her tumbling hair. Tenderness flashed over his features. 'Give me one now, Caro, and my God, I'll come to you like a rocket.'

He had put it into words, all her growing wariness enforced by what he said. Maggie had known this; Jake had been hinting at it. Slowly she had come to suspect it. Now she knew and she looked at him with puzzled, doubtful eyes.

Uncertainly she murmured, 'It's too soon, Jake ... far too soon.'

He sighed. 'If you say so.'

'Give me time,' she said, but her voice held a strange tremulousness, because the way his eyes were eating her face was having its own effect, and she could feel her heartbeats racing away.

He looked at her, sighed again. 'Mmm,' he murmured, leaning forward. His mouth touched hers lightly, then hardened, then they were kissing with a strange, hot need which shook Caroline to her roots, because now she was not merely accepting his passion, she was returning it, and they both knew it.

They stood there kissing, pressing closer together, and she lost count of time. She was altogether lost, wandering in a daze, responsive to his hands and body and mouth, mindlessly submitting, needing it.

Other guests arrived and the sound of their car broke them out of the sensuous dream. Jake pulled away, his features blind in the car headlights, and Caroline felt her own heart beating wildly, her breathing ragged and uneven.

He laughed huskily. 'My God!'

She turned away, flustered, and Jake caught her hand. 'Don't look so panic-stricken,' he said teasingly. 'I won't hold it against you. So you caved in ... it's no crime!' Then, his smile mocking, 'I have that effect on women, didn't you know?'

'You've told me often enough,' she retorted, trying to catch the lightness of his tone. He was trying to pass the moment without making too much of it, she saw. He was making it easy for them both to go on into the lights and noise of the party. They were neither of them in a condition to walk into a room full of people. Jake was a damned good actor, but he couldn't hide the look on his face at the moment, any more than she could. They had both been swept away and it showed. Even strangers could see it, she suspected.

The other people were flooding past them, eyeing them with curious amusement, and the door opened and light fell out in a yellow river over them all. Simone welcomed them, tall and elegiac in a purple dress which looked perfect on her but which would look odd on anyone else. She had a personal style which was compelling.

She kissed Jake's cheek, patting him, then gave Caroline a long, interested look. 'We must have a long chat later,' she told her. 'We're going to have a lot in common.' She looked from Caroline's flushed, brilliant-eyed face to Jake and her brows rose steeply, a smile lifting the corners of her mouth. 'Sure you want to stay for the party?' Her clever, sophisticated eyes mocked Jake. 'I get the distinct impression you two would be better off alone.'

Jake's skin darkened with colour and he gave Simone a look which held no answering amusement. 'Miss your party, darling? As if we could!'

Simone made a little moue of wry amusement at him. 'Sorry if I touched a delicate spot,' she teased. 'Take Caro in and find her a drink, darling—and, Jake ...'

He turned his dishevelled, rakish head, his black brows lifted. 'Yes?'

'Try not to look so wound-up,' Simone said softly. 'You might as well wear a label.'

'Go to hell,' Jake growled, pulling Caroline into the long room where the party was centred.

After Simone's knowledgeable mockery, they both tried to look cool and offhand, but what had happened earlier was making them far too aware of each other and it showed. People tended to look from one to the other of them with curious faces and then to do a vanishing act, discretion being the better part of valour. Nobody, Caroline thought, wanted to stand between them, as though a laser lance cut from one to the other and anyone in the way might get burnt up, because that was what it felt like to her, as though she were on fire.

They danced, and her body was unbearably, intolerantly sensitive as though Jake's lightest fingertip touch could start a blaze in her. Jake seemed spare of words. He used them grittily, biting them out, and he wasn't looking at her. He wasn't looking

at anything. He was rigid, like a man in pain, and
she knew exactly what was eating him because it was
eating her too.

'This is a turn-up for the book,' he muttered as
they stopped dancing and took a drink. 'Let me take
you away from here, Caro.'

She looked up at him dazedly and might have
said yes except that her eye caught a flicker of movement behind him; she looked past to find herself
looking at James, and the shock made her whiten
and gasp.

Jake thought the gasp and the draining of her
colour was for what he had said. He groaned, laying
a hand on her hip, his fingers spread wide, stroking
her. 'Darling, don't play around with me, not now.
We both know what's going on between us.'

She wasn't even listening. She was looking at
James and James was looking back, white with rage,
his eyes black with unspoken temper and his mouth
shaking.

While they were staring at each other across the
noisy room a woman came up to James and handed
him a glass, frowned, followed his fixed stare and
did an obvious double-take. The recognition was
mutual. Caroline had seen her once before, in
James's office, in James's arms, and her eyes went
through Linda Blare with immediate, bitter hostility, then flicked contemptuously to James. He
had brought the woman to the party, yet he stood
there, showing anger because she was with Jake!
How two-faced could you get? Who did he think
he was? There were double standards, were there,
one for him and one for her! That was what he
thought.

She turned her eyes back to Jake who was looking down at her in angry silence.

'What,' he asked through his teeth, 'is he doing here? Did you tell him I'd be here?'

'No,' she said. 'I imagine Simone invited him. He was lunching with her the day we met her.'

Jake looked taken aback at that. 'Was he? He knows Simone?' He glanced across the room at the distinctive, elegant figure of Simone. 'How come, I wonder?'

'Why not ask her?' she suggested drily.

'I'll do that,' he said, taking her arm. 'Come along.'

Simone greeted them charmingly, smiling at them both. 'I saw you dancing together,' she said, eyes glinting. 'Delightful ... what world were you in, I wonder?'

Jake ignored that. 'How come James Fox is here tonight?' he asked.

Simone looked puzzled. 'I invited him,' she said, lifting one brow. 'Why not?'

'How come you know him?'

'He's taking a case for me,' she explained. Her eyes flashed. 'A libel case ... he thinks I've got a good case against the trash-hound who slandered me.' She talked about the case she was bringing against a newspaper and Jake listened, interested from a professional point of view, forgetting his anger over James's presence.

'He's a good barrister,' Simone ended calmly. 'No?'

'He's also Caro's husband,' said Jake in bald tones.

Simone turned her head and stared at Caroline. 'Oh, my God!' She touched Jake's arm apologetically. 'Darling, I'd no idea . . . if I had, I would never have invited him tonight! You did tell me she was married, but not to whom.'

'Forget it,' Jake shrugged. 'So long as he doesn't make trouble.'

Simone looked interested. 'He might?' She glanced across at James and her eyes twinkled. 'He looks far too controlled for that. And he's brought one of his partners with him, so he isn't likely to do anything to cause talk while she's around.'

As if her glance had activated him, James was walking over to them, Linda Blare beside him. Jake bristled, his arm sliding around Caroline's waist. James looked at Simone, ignoring them. 'A delightful party,' he said, and the sound of his deep, cool voice touched something in Caroline's mind, making her jerk physically, as though a nerve had been plucked. Jake felt it and looked down at her, brows frowning.

Simone was amused now. The twist in the situation was just the sort of joke to touch her sense of humour. 'You know Caroline, of course,' she said, tongue in cheek. 'And Jake.'

She might just as well have laughed out loud, and James detested being laughed at; it would drive him mad for her to know that his wife was with another man. He was looking at Jake with a peculiarly rigid face and she could see a tiny muscle jumping in his cheek. Jake acted like mad. He gave James a lazy, insolent smile. 'We've bumped into each other,' he said, and the hinted reference to the day James had knocked him down was mocking. Then Jake glanced at Linda Blare and lifted his famous brows in a charming smile. 'We haven't met, though,' he

added, implying that he would remember it if they
had, and Linda Blare smiled, involuntarily, as
though she couldn't help herself.

'Linda, this is Jake Redway,' said James as if he
detested introducing them. Linda offered her hand
and Jake lifted it to his lips and kissed it with a
courtly bow which stopped short of being mockery.

James moved his eyes slowly to Caroline. 'My
wife,' he said brusquely.

Linda turned her head and looked at Caroline
who looked back, a cold defiance in her face. She
had not yet looked at her rival properly, but she
looked now, and found it unsurprising that James
had fallen for her. She was exactly the type for him.
Her face was not beautiful, but it held intelligence
and shrewdness, and her brown hair was glossy, like
a shiny chestnut. She was older than Caroline, perhaps in her thirties. They stared at each other and
were curious, each knowing that the other was making a close inspection.

Several other people had drifted up, among them
a film producer who hailed Jake eagerly; fixing on
to him with a spate of words. Jake had to turn away
from them, listening politely, and somehow Simone
moved away, leaving Caroline isolated with James
and Linda Blare. Somehow without being rude she
had to get away from them, but Linda Blare was
speaking to her calmly, politely, and she had to
answer her questions because there was no good
reason why she should not. 'Yes, I was an actress
once.'

'You met Mr Redway at drama school?'

'Yes,' said Caroline, glancing briefly, coldly at
James. 'We are old friends.'

James muttered something about getting another drink and vanished. Linda Blare said quietly, 'Can we move somewhere quieter? I have to talk to you, Mrs Fox.'

Caroline looked at her, hesitated, but complied. They moved into a spot near the open windows which led on to a small terrace balcony. A few people were out there, smoking, the tips of their cigarettes little red lights in the dark sky.

Linda Blare watched Caroline thoughtfully for a moment. 'James has told me you want a divorce,' she said.

'Did he?' Caroline wanted to hit her. She looked at the cool, contained face and felt anger like a flame inside her.

'You can't,' Linda Blare said abruptly.

'What?' Caroline could hardly believe her ears. She stared furiously at the other woman.

'At this juncture in his career it would be a mortal blow,' Linda Blare said. 'He's working towards his silk—you know that. Any scandal could be fatal; at best it would be a disadvantage. Surely you realise James has ambitions of being a judge one day? A divorce could put a stop to that for good.'

Caroline gave her a long, bewildered look. 'You're urging me not to get a divorce?' She had expected Linda Blare to be all in favour of that idea; after all, she wanted James to be free. Why was she opposing it now?

'Yes, of course.' There was an impatient note in the other's voice. 'James has worked so hard and he deserves his silk. It would be a crying shame if he missed this chance because of talk over his marriage. To be able to write Q.C. after his name is one of the dreams of any barrister, and with James it won't stop there. He's good, really good, and he's going to the top.'

'Does he know you're speaking to me about it?' Caroline frowned, watching her intelligent, cool face.

'No,' Linda said quickly. 'No.'

'If he knew don't you think he might be angry?' Caroline kept a light note in her voice, forcing down the jealous rage she was feeling.

'Furious!' Linda looked rueful. 'It's none of my business, I know that. But you must see that, quite apart from a personal respect and admiration for James, I have the future of the chambers on my mind ... having a Q.C. on our list can do us nothing but good.'

Caroline was confused, puzzled. The other woman was talking about James in a way which did not suggest the sort of emotional involvement which Caroline knew she must feel. Eyeing her, Caroline decided she must be a superb actress. 'Perhaps James would consider the sacrifice worth while,' she said, and knew her jealousy was audible in her tense voice.

'I know he loves you deeply, but isn't that a rather selfish way of looking at it?' Linda was staring at her with scornful dislike, but her words were so astonishing that Caroline was too taken aback to think about that.

'I'm not a fool,' she burst out. 'I know about you!'

Open-mouthed, Linda looked back at her and even Caroline could not believe now that her shocked amazement was anything but genuine.

'Me? What on earth are you talking about?'

'James and ... you ...' Caroline said very slowly.

'You're mad!' exclaimed Linda Blare with an affronted look. 'Mad or very cunning ... there's nothing between myself and James! He's confided in me now and then, it's true. Since I was another woman, he thought I might advise him about ...' Her voice broke off and her face grew softer, her eyes looking at Caroline with faint concern. 'Mrs Fox, I'm a married woman myself, I have two children ... didn't James ever tell you?'

Perhaps he had, Caroline thought dazedly, but she had never heard him, she had never listened. She was shivering, her brain racing round in wild circles.

'I was so sorry about your accident, the baby ... I know what a terrible blow it must have been. James was out of his mind that day. I was desperately sorry for him. It was then that he told me about you for the first time. He was so worried and unhappy.'

All the things she had overheard when she visited James's office could have a totally different explanation, Caroline realised. She had added two and two and made five, but then looks had been deceptive.

Linda Blare was staring at her, a slight smile on her face now. 'You surely never really suspected James of ...'

Caroline flushed. 'I'm sorry, it was stupid of me. I overheard him talking to you one day and I misunderstood.'

'That wasn't why you were divorcing him?' Alarm flashed into the other woman's clever face. 'My God!'

Caroline said bitterly, 'Was it so surprising?

Obviously you would make him a better wife than
I ever have.'

'Like isn't always attracted to like,' Linda Blare
confessed drily. 'My husband is an engineer ...
splendid with his hands, he can make any piece of
machinery run as smoothly as silk, but it's no use
asking him for conversation. He confines what he
says to the fewest possible words. I often ask myself
what I saw in him, but that's the way love works
sometimes.'

'After two years of marriage James and I are total
strangers,' Caroline confessed, and was angry with
herself for being so frank with a stranger.

'Poor James,' said Linda slowly, her eyes dis-
mayed. 'Are you still going to divorce him? Please,
reconsider ... it would truly come at the worst possible moment.'

'I don't want to hurt his career,' Caroline said
dully. 'No, I shan't divorce him.'

CHAPTER SIX

CAROLINE could not stand it for another second. She
had to get away from Linda Blare, out of this over-
crowded, noisy room full of strangers. She turned
and walked away with a muttered excuse of some
kind. She barely knew what she was saying; her
mind was too full of the realisation that all her as-

sumptions about James had been wrong. Wrong again. Was she always going to be wrong about him?

She looked for Jake and saw him in the centre of a lively, laughing group of people, all of whom were strangers to her, except Simone Corona. She did not think she could face Jake at the moment. Quietly she slid past and went out into the night.

It was chilly. She pulled her thin shawl up around her shoulders, shivering, and leaned on a lamp-post in the yellow circle of light, head bent.

James had not been in love with Linda Blare; the other woman's angry certainty had convinced her beyond a doubt. She had jumped to a conclusion which was false.

She thought back to that morning, the confused events of which were kaleidoscoping in her mind. She had woken up with a sensation of restless energy. For months her waking mood had been so different, one of dull depression, a weariness, lassitude, a disinclination to do anything. She should have realised that morning that something had altered inside her, but she had been so used to her grey fog of misery that she had not even realised when it began to lift.

James had gone to work. She had suddenly decided to go up to London, and that alone should have told her that something had changed. She had made a decision to act. Deep in the confines of her subconscious something had been happening, perhaps for days, and it had surfaced that morning. She had acted on it without considering what she was doing, but now looking back she knew that she had wanted to break the mould which had held her for months. She had wanted to be restored to life.

So she had gone to London and met Maggie, and through Maggie's eyes seen herself as she had become—a lost woman, grim, dull, defeated. And the sight had angered her.

She had secretly blamed James—she knew that very well. Before her marriage to him she had been full of life, so she had blamed him for what had become of her during her marriage to him. She had gone to find him, though, still intending to ask him to try again, to make their marriage work, and she had seen him with Linda Blare, and misunderstood what he said.

Perhaps, she thought grimly, she had even wanted to believe that he no longer loved her. Perhaps she had jumped at the idea that he cared for someone else.

Their relationship had been so tortuous by then, so ravaged by feelings of inadequacy on her part, guilt, resentment and failure to communicate, that somewhere in her mind, she suspected, she had wanted to end it all, the humiliating, painful tangle of love and bitterness.

She held the shawl across her breast, shuddering. Love ... did she still love him? She did not even know for sure. After tonight—and Jake.

A car swept down the road and the headlights flashed over the pavement. She heard a slight movement behind her and turned, nerves jumping. A leaf blowing in the wind; a cat or dog slinking past? Her eyes searched the darkness and she gave a faint cry as she saw a figure lurking near the doorway.

'It's all right,' he said, coming forward slowly. 'It's only me.'

Alarm made her angry. 'Why were you skulking about there? You frightened me!'

'That was what I didn't want to do,' he said grimly. 'I was keeping out of sight.'

Caroline twisted the ends of the shawl between her hands. 'What are you doing out here?'

'Watching you,' he said.

Their eyes met through the shadows. 'Why did you come out here?' he asked, moving closer.

'I wanted some air. And to think.'

'About what?' He was beside her, his lean figure dwarfing her, and she felt her breath sucked into her lungs with a sort of protest.

'Don't worry,' he said bitterly. 'Rape isn't on my mind.'

'That's a relief,' she said in tones as savage, and they glared at each other.

Then he pushed his hands into his pockets, squaring his shoulders. 'Caro, I'm sorry.' His voice was urgent, low. 'I wish to God I hadn't done that.'

'So do I,' she said fervently.

'Yes,' he muttered, head bent. 'You provoked me to it ... you realise that? I'm not made of stone.'

'Aren't you? I thought you were.'

He lifted his head and the grey eyes were silvery with emotion. 'Did you have to tell me about Redway? Do you think the fear of him coming back hadn't been in my mind for years? It was like standing on a railway track watching a train flashing towards you and being unable to stop what you knew was going to happen.'

Once she might have been fierce with contradiction, disputing that she had ever seen Jake as anything but a friend, but not now, not after tonight. Jake had shown her conclusively that she had been wrong about him, too. She was wrong about everyone, everything. She had been blind to herself as much as to everyone else. She had never known what she did feel, and even now she was baffled by the tangle of her own emotions.

Her silence made James tense, staring at her. She looked up at him and said quietly, 'If I divorced you now it could make problems for you, couldn't it? A divorce would put a black mark against you as far as getting your silk is concerned.'

He watched her, frowning. 'Possibly, but I expect I would weather that.'

'It would be best to wait, though,' she said, slightly uncertain, looking at him, trying to read his mind, but then had she ever managed to read his mind? Had she ever come anywhere near it? She had never guessed that he was jealous of Jake, and yet now she was sure he had been, all through their marriage, and he had successfully hidden that from her.

He was watching her searchingly. 'Linda said something to you,' he suggested, and she half smiled. He had always been too quick for her, reading her thoughts before she knew them herself.

'It should have occurred to me,' she said.

'Linda had no right!'

'She had every right. She works with you; she knows the effect a divorce can have.'

'It isn't a crime these days.'

'It isn't smiled on, though.' She looked at him, her mouth lifting in a little smile. 'Not for judges.'

James, astonishingly, smiled, too. 'Not for judges,' he agreed drily.

'And you want to be a judge.'

'I suppose I fancy myself in ermine,' he drawled, and his tone was humorous, self-mocking.

Caroline shivered in a sudden blast of icy wind and he tentatively put a finger on her shoulder. 'You're cold out here. You ought to go back inside.'

'No,' she said quickly, 'I couldn't.'

He frowned. 'Is something wrong?' His eyes searched her face. 'Have you quarrelled with Redway?'

'No,' she said. 'I ... I'm just not in the mood for a crowd.'

He paused for a moment, then asked, 'Would you like to drive around for a while? My car is over there.'

She glanced away, then looked back at him. 'Take me home, James,' she said huskily.

His eyes narrowed and she felt the tension rising in his body. 'Why?' he asked her curtly.

'We have to talk,' she said. 'We can't talk here, or anywhere ... except there.'

There was a silence while he stared across the dark, windy street. 'And Redway?'

'Please!' she begged, and he shrugged.

'Very well.'

In the car she leaned back, shivering, and he switched on the heater, sending a waft of warm air over her legs. 'Better?'

'Much,' she said, cuddling down in comfort.

'That dress is very sexy but not practical,' said James, and again she heard the faint note of humour in his deep voice.

'It wasn't intended for walking the streets in,' she confessed, and he laughed outright.

'It could cause a riot,' he said.

Another of those dreadful silences came after that and she stared at the unwinding road, wondering how she was going to find the words to talk to him.

'Are you in love with Redway?' he asked suddenly, not looking at her.

It was the opening she wanted and she knew it. 'I don't know,' she muttered, watching his dark profile.

His mouth compressed. 'Still? My God, Caroline, what does it take to make you certain of anything?'

'I've never been very good at reading my own motives,' she said. 'I was so bad at it that I didn't even know how bad I was.'

'Do you know how often you mentioned him to me even before we were married? I got sick of the sound of his name.'

'You never said anything.'

'I wasn't going to make a fool of myself,' he said curtly. 'Jealous scenes are contemptible.'

'I had no idea you were jealous.'

'Thank God,' he said roughly. 'I despise myself enough as it is.'

'Because of what happened the other night?'

He changed gear violently and the car shuddered. 'That and other things,' he said.

'James, if we don't talk we'll never come to an understanding,' Caroline said desperately.

He glanced at her quickly. 'Is that what you want? What do you mean, an understanding?'

She gave a groan of self-despair. 'I'm not even sure about that.'

He stared ahead, his features rigid. 'If you're asking me to turn a blind eye while you have an affair with Redway and work him out of your system, the answer is no, Caroline.' He turned his head and his eyes were savage. 'I'd kill you first.'

'A drastic solution,' she said, and he made a sound deep in his throat.

'Don't laugh at me, Caro.'

She sighed. 'I'm not ... at myself, perhaps.'

'I don't find any of this remotely funny.'

'Neither do I,' she said. 'We've never understood each other, and it hasn't all been my fault. You froze me out months ago, even before the baby.'

The car leaped forward, his hands tightening on the wheel. 'I'm sorry about the baby,' he said huskily. 'I've blamed myself ever since. I behaved like a swine over it and I've regretted it.'

'Can we talk about that? About why you refused to have a child?'

'I told you,' he said, but she watched him and saw his bones tighten under the austere skin.

'James, we've got to have the truth before we can understand each other,' she said. 'Why didn't you want me to have a child?'

He was silent, his face averted.

'James,' she whispered, laying a hand on his knee, and he jumped as though she had struck him.

'Don't!' he said hoarsely, and she realised his hands were shaking on the wheel.

She sat back, perturbed. There was another long tense silence. He gave a rough sigh, almost a groan.

'I was jealous.' The words were ground out as though he barely opened his teeth to let them pass.

'Sickeningly jealous. I didn't want you to have anyone else in your life.'

'Even your own child?' She was aghast, although Maggie had already put the thought into her mind.

'I know,' he said harshly. 'It's contemptible—do you think I don't know that? Do you think I wanted to feel like that? I couldn't do a thing about the way I felt. I tried, God knows I tried. I threw myself into my work to try to escape from the endless circle of my need for you, but it made no difference. You were in my mind night and day and I knew damned well I wasn't in yours—the very fact that you wanted a child proved that. You didn't find me sufficient to fill your life. You were always looking outwards, at other people, other things ... Redway, the theatre, people you'd met ... and then the idea of having a child.'

She gently said, 'It's normal to have a family, James.'

He laughed bitterly. 'And I'm not? I'm aware of it. Don't you understand? I wanted nothing but you. You, you, you ...' His voice was wild with an emotion she found painful and disturbing. He didn't even look at her, driving as though he barely knew she was there, yet she could feel the obsessive tentacles of his passion reaching out towards her now, and she was numb with realisation and bewilderment.

'You never showed me any of this.'

'Of course I didn't,' he bit out. 'I have my pride. The last thing I wanted was for you to realise how I felt. It was easier to let you think I was indifferent than to have you know I was insane about you.'

She trembled, linking her fingers together. 'If I'd known I could have ...'

'What?' he asked. 'Been sorry for me? Pacified me, humoured me? Do you think I wanted that? That would have been worse than anything.'

And so, strangled with pride and self-contempt, he had struggled against his feelings for months, never letting her see beneath the cold, arrogant surface, shutting her out, building that wall between them which had finally driven her away from him.

'You're a fool, James,' she said, and he gave her a bitter look.

'About you, yes, from the day we met. From the beginning I knew I had Redway's ghost to contend with—his name was never off your lips, and I was so jealous I could have killed you, then, but you went on seeing me and when I asked you to marry me, you accepted, so I jumped at my chance and got you before he could come back.'

'You had it wrong,' she said. 'Jake was never anything more than my friend then.'

'No woman talks that much about a man unless he's more than her friend,' James said savagely.

'Well, I wasn't aware of anything else,' she sighed.

They drew up at their home and she looked at the darkened windows. They were like her life with James, shuttered, secretive, dark. Somehow she had to fling the windows open and then she might see clearly what it was she wanted.

She switched on the central heating and began to make coffee while he put the car away. James walked into the room and stood, watching her, his hands in his pockets.

'Do you want anything to eat?' she asked, attempting a normal tone.

'No, thank you. Coffee will do.'

She poured it and added cream, watching it swirl in marbled rings over the dark surface.

They sat down at the polished pine table and he stared into his cup, stirring the spoon round and round aimlessly.

'He's your lover now,' he said in clipped tones which no longer hid from her the tortured emotion beneath.

'No,' she said and he lifted his head to stare at her, eyes narrowed.

'Not yet,' she said, because everything had to be clear and plain between them now, and saw him wince.

'Is that what you've come here to talk about?' He sounded like a man pushed to his limit and she reached across the table and touched his hand. He pulled it away as if she had put a hot iron on his skin.

'Don't touch me,' he said through his teeth. 'My God, can't you get it into your head? I'm not normal where you're concerned. Last time I lost my mind I hurt you badly enough, but I'm afraid that one day I'll kill you.'

She tried for lightness, to bring him down from the bitter plane on which he was existing. 'Worked out your method yet?'

He looked at her as if she was mad and she smiled pleadingly.

'Oh, no,' he said then, soberly enough. 'Every time I think about it I know very well how it would end ... if I got my hands on you I'd have other things than murder on my mind.'

Caroline felt her skin flushing and looked away because he was no longer putting up any barriers between them and his eyes were eating her. 'Didn't it ever occur to you that I might think you no longer loved me?' she asked huskily.

'You couldn't have thought that!'

'I did,' she said, her eyes on the table. 'I even thought there was someone else.'

A silence, then James asked flatly, 'Did that bother you?'

'Yes,' she said.

He got up and walked away, the lean body bent as though in a high wind. 'Until you met Redway again,' he said, but there was a faint question in his voice.

'That's what we have to talk about,' she said, and he swung round, face white.

'If you're going to him, go ... and stay out of my life!'

'It isn't that simple,' she sighed. 'You were right in a way. Jake did mean more to me than I ever realised. I still don't know how much.'

'I don't want to hear about it,' said James.

'That's it, though,' she said. 'We've never talked to each other. You hid your feelings from me all along and guessed about mine ... and I had no idea how I felt. Isn't it time we had some plain speaking? The only way to straighten out the mess we've made of our lives is to be frank.'

He walked to the table and poured himself another cup of coffee. 'I need a whisky,' he said, putting it down, and vanished. He came back with the decanter and a glass and poured a stiff whisky. Caroline watched as he swallowed it. The alcohol brought a faint flush to his hard cheekbones.

He sat down, pouring another drink. 'Very well, Caroline. If you want me to listen, I'll listen.'

'It honestly never occurred to me that Jake meant any more to me than a friend,' she said. 'Now, I'm not sure ... I'm confused. You and Jake between you have confused me. You locked too much of your feelings and thoughts inside yourself, James. I didn't have any idea of all this, nor did it occur to me that I could do a thing about the way our marriage was breaking up.'

James watched her over his glass, his eyes shuttered. 'Isn't it Redway you should be talking to, not me? He's in love with you—I knew that when I met him. That isn't just my obsession talking ... I'm a trained observer and I took a good, hard look at Redway. He was hiding nothing from me and I knew he wanted you.'

'Yes,' she said, 'he does. He showed me that to-night and I should have known it before, but in his way Jake was as secretive as you are ... he hid it from me for a long time because he knew I wasn't aware of him in that way.'

'Now you are?'

'Yes,' she said, meeting his eyes.

He smiled tightly. 'Then there's no problem.'

'There is,' she said. 'I've been totally lacking in self-awareness until now, but I'm waking up with a vengeance. During the last six months of our marriage we lived as strangers and when I came out of my fog I needed warmth. Jake was there to give it to me and it woke me up to what had been between us for a long, long time without my realising it. But that doesn't make things simple, James. It complicates things.'

'Why?' he asked, frowning.

'Because there's you,' she said.

'There's no need to feel guilty about me,' he said flatly. 'I'm not going to say I'll get over you, because I know I never shall, but I'm not going to keep you out of a sense of guilt. What sort of marriage could we have with that for a foundation? If you want Redway, go to him.'

'You haven't understood me,' she said patiently. 'Guilt doesn't come into it. It's my own needs I don't understand.'

His eyes flashed. 'Make yourself clearer, Caroline.'

'You know what I'm saying,' she said, staring at him.

'Put it in black and white, for God's sake!'

'I want both of you,' she said.

James stood up, his chair crashing to the floor. 'No!' he said fiercely. 'Never in this life ... my God, what do you think I am? I'm not sharing you with Redway.'

'That wasn't what I meant,' she sighed, shaking her head. 'I'm not asking you to share anything. I'm asking you to wait.'

'While you sate yourself with him?' The question was brutally sharp, bitter. 'No, Caroline. Oh, no.'

She stood up too, struggling for a way to explain to him. 'While I find out what I feel,' she said. 'James, I don't intend to make Jake my lover, I swear to you.'

'No,' he gritted. 'No! I'm not even going to discuss it. You'd better go, Caroline, before I lose my temper.'

'What shall I do?' she asked drily. 'Walk to London?'

He stood with his back to her. 'You can use your old room, if you like, but go to bed now, please. I want to be alone.'

'May I use the phone first? I should ring Maggie and let her know I'm safe.'

'Thoughtful of you,' he said sarcastically. 'You didn't do me the same favour the night you walked out on me. I sat here all night waiting to hear you'd been killed under a train or in a car.'

'I'm sorry about that,' she said. 'James, I am sorry . . . there were reasons why I didn't ring.'

'I bet there were!'

'I was under the impression you wouldn't care if I never came back,' she said bitterly.

He laughed coldly. 'I wish to God I had been that indifferent. I went through hell.'

Caroline hesitated, looking at the averted dark head, then she went out and rang Maggie.

'You're where?' Maggie's voice rose furiously. 'Are you out of your mind? What are you playing at?'

'I had to talk to him.'

'Jake has been here,' Maggie told her. 'Frantic because you'd vanished with him.'

'Could you let him know I'm safe?'

'But are you?' Maggie was very angry. 'Do you think it will calm Jake down to know you're under the same roof as James Fox?'

'I'll talk to Jake myself tomorrow,' Caroline said.

'Caroline, at times you make me livid!' Maggie flung the phone down, and Caroline sighed.

She heard sardonic laughter and turned to find James behind her, his eyes bitterly amused. 'Well, now he knows what it's like,' he commented.

'Goodnight, James,' she murmured, and left him there, watching her as she climbed the stairs. It was a strange experience to undress in her old room. She felt as though she had not been in it for centuries, but it was only a short time. It was crowded with grey memories of past unhappiness and she shivered in it, beset by them. I hate this room, she thought. It reminds me of too many things I want to forget. Maybe it would be wiser to forget her marriage along with them, but she knew she couldn't do that.

She had to sort out her real emotions, separate the confused tangle of motivations and somehow decide what she really wanted out of life. She had rushed into her marriage without having any real idea of the man she was marrying or of her own feelings about him. James had hidden too much from her, complicating what was already complicated enough. Jealousy was not an emotion she had ever thought about much, but if she had she would have seen it as a hot, fierce feeling, not as the cold, obsessive thing James had shown her it could be.

Until she had made sure about her feelings for Jake, though, she could not know how she felt about James.

Tonight Jake had swept her off her feet. The old image of him she had carried around for so long had no connection with the man she had discovered to-night as he held her in her arms. Feeling like this, she could not resume her marriage with James.

She could not settle. She felt like a cat in a strange house. She wandered around the room, opening cupboards, staring at objects in drawers. They were all her own things, and that was what they were ... things, without meaning for her in her present state, objects frozen in a timeless ice, fossilised in the past. Her clothes hung in the wardrobe; the drawers were packed with her lingerie. She ran her cold fingers through them, the silk and lace slipping over her skin, and they might have belonged to someone else.

Pulling on a wrap, she went downstairs again and James stood up and came out to stare at her. 'What's wrong now?'

'I want a drink,' she said. 'To help me sleep.'

Silently he poured her a glass of brandy and she took it in both hands, as though it might warm her, but her body was ice-cold and the glass on her skin made her shiver. She looked down into the liquid, whirling it round, watching it closely.

'Go to bed,' said James curtly, turning away, as he had done so many times over the last year, but now the ice in his voice could not cover his real feelings and she watched his tall, lean body with a dry mouth.

'I can't sleep in that room,' she said. 'It reminds me of too much I want to forget.'

'What do you suggest?' he asked caustically. 'That you sleep with me? If you do, you'll take the consequences.'

She looked at him through her lashes and knew it was what she wanted. She wanted him to break through the wall of ice and make her blood rush round her body again, make her human. Everything in this house crushed her. It pressed down on her like pack ice, chilling and defeating her.

He turned and their eyes met and she knew he could read her mind. His face stiffened and he slowly came over to her. She stood there, shivering slightly, the brandy glass between her hands. James took it and raised it to her mouth. 'Drink it,' he said quite gently.

She swallowed, grimacing. 'Vile taste!'

He tilted it again and she drank again, feeling the heat flush through her veins, her cheeks bloom with sudden life. James put the glass down on the table and looked at her through his long, dark lashes, a secretive brooding in his eyes.

'I could take you up on your offer,' he said carefully. 'But if I did I wouldn't let you go again, Caro. I've come to the limit of my ability to stand punishment. It's up to you.'

She looked down, remembering her own reaction in Jake's arms, and torn by indecision. Before she could go to James she had to know precisely how she felt about Jake.

'We still haven't talked it out,' she said. 'Things couldn't go on the way they did before. You say you object to my needing other people ... but I do, James. I like having friends around me, I love the stage, I want to work again. Marriage doesn't have to be a case of one man, one life.'

She saw the savagery in his eyes and said quickly, 'No, I'm not suggesting extra-marital affairs. I'm talking about a lot of other things. Our marriage could have been so different if we had stayed in London, where we're both at home, where I could have seen my friends, gone to the theatre occasionally ...'

'Seen Redway?' His question tore into her, jealousy unveiled in all its icy cruelty, his eyes leaping with it.

'Do you honestly think it was Jake alone I missed?' She sighed, weary of the circular discussion. 'It was so many other things I barely know where to start. This house—oh, it's beautiful, but for me it's always been a prison—I never realised how much of one until tonight. You locked me up here and threw away the key.'

His hands took hold of her upper arms, digging into her flesh. 'I've had enough. Go to bed, Caroline.'

She looked up at him defiantly. 'That is how you've spoken to me for months ... as if I were a halfwit or a child, using your court voice on me, dismissing me ...'

'For good reason,' he said through his teeth, his eyes flickering between their long lashes.

She dropped her lids, thinking. 'If we tried again, I'd want a whole new set of rules.'

His fingers tightened. 'Such as?'

'We sell this house,' she said. 'Get a flat in London. I get a job. We try ... try, James, to communicate.'

He was watching her intently, his face unreadable. 'And Redway?'

She lifted her eyes to his face. 'No Jake,' she said. 'Obviously, no Jake.'

He drew a long, shaken breath. His hands lifted from her shoulders, touched her face, his fingers stroking her hair back from her temples.

'And me?' he asked huskily. 'What do you feel for

me, Caro? You make all this sound like a business proposition.'

She laid her hands on his chest, pressing them against him, feeling his heart leaping under them. Leaning forward, she touched her mouth softly against his throat and his arms came round her, holding her. They pressed together, silently, a peculiar waiting between them. James laid his cheek against hers, one hand stroking her hair.

'Be patient, James,' she whispered. 'Give me time—a trial run.'

'You ask a good deal,' he said drily, still stroking her hair. 'I'm barely able to keep my hands off you now.'

'So long as you tell me about it,' she said, slightly teasing him.

'I'll tell you,' he said in husky tones. 'Night and day, if you're prepared to listen.'

'I'll listen,' she promised. 'I've had enough of long silences. We'll talk all night if you want to.'

'I have better things to do with my nights,' he said, and she gave a little smile.

'First we must talk.' She yawned, covering her mouth with her hand lazily. 'I'm tired. Shall we go to bed?'

He contemplated her from beneath his hooded lids. 'Together?'

She openly teased him now. 'Are you against the idea?'

'No,' he said. 'For it.' His hand slowly stroked down her back. 'Oh, God, Caroline, for it.'

'Keep me warm, James,' she whispered, head against his shoulder.

They went upstairs and he lit the twin lamps on
either side of their double bed. Caroline snuggled
down under the warm bedclothes and waited for
him, going into his arms with a long sigh when he
joined her. Her head on his body, she settled to
sleep and heard him breathing slowly and regularly
below her head, his hands touching her softly, without pressure, as though all he needed to know was
that she was there. For the first time in many months
she went to sleep with a smile on her mouth, knowing she was safe, feeling herself loved.

CHAPTER SEVEN

SHE woke in the morning and it was raining, the
windows running with it, the soft ceaseless sound of
it filling the air, but she was lying in James's arms,
cradled on his body, and she was warm and content.
She snuggled against him and his arms tightened so
that she knew he was awake, too, and turned her
cheek against him to look up at him. From this
angle she could see the Celtic bone structure of his
face like the scaffolding of a house, stark and strong,
the long jawline hard above the sharp line of his
mouth.

'What day is it?' Caroline asked sleepily, and he
gave a strange little smile, as though the irrelevance
of the question amused him.

'Sunday,' he said. 'In a minute the church bells will start.'

'I'm hungry,' she said, stretching, and his hand stole up the curve of her back, fingering the line of her body as though he found a sensual pleasure in the touch of her.

'I don't know what there is to eat,' he said, frowning.

'Haven't you been eating?' She glanced up at him and his hand wove into her hair, fingering the strands, lifting and dropping them gently.

Their eyes held and Caroline felt her heart begin to beat fast. The bodily warmth between them was making her languorous, a deep relaxation covering her. She remembered the long nights of the first months of their marriage and James's passion, the force of which had carried her helpless in his arms. She dropped her head weakly against his shoulder, her mouth against the skin laid bare by his pyjamas.

His hand tugged at her hair, pulling back her head, and his mouth slowly, slowly approached her lips, as if he was giving her time to withdraw, to reject.

She watched the hard line of his face through lowered lashes, aching. His mouth touched hers so lightly it was like the brush of a lash on her skin. She breathed carefully, as though afraid she might frighten him away, as though he were a timid animal stealing up to her. Her hand came up and clasped his cheek, cupping it, holding it against her, and then the pressure changed. He was trembling, she felt the movement in her own body. His lips hardened and her own parted under them, admitting him, submitting. She touched the tip of her

tongue delicately against his mouth, watching him
through her lashes, seeing a flush grow on his cheekbones, hearing him groan.

A moment later she was flung across the bed, his
body following her, and they kissed hungrily, an
explosive desire openly between them now. She
wound her arms round his neck, mouth open, shuddering.

'You want me ... do you want me?' The muttered words were barely coherent, thickly groaned
into her ear as he kissed the bare warm curve of her
neck, following it from her ear to the hollow in her
shoulder, covering her skin with light kisses, brushing, tantalising.

Before she could answer the telephone rang. The
sound made them both jump violently, they were so
sunk in absorption with each other.

James froze, swearing under his breath.

'Who the hell can that be?'

The same thought came into both their minds.
They looked at each other and Caroline bit her lip.

'Redway,' James said tightly.

'It could be,' she admitted, her voice still husky
with the passion she had felt.

'Damn him to hell,' he muttered, leaping out of
the bed. He went to the telephone and picked it up.

'Yes?' he barked into the receiver.

She watched the hard, dark mask of his face and
knew it was Jake. He flung the telephone down and
turned to look at her. She climbed out of the bed
and went towards him, feeling his eyes on her every
step of the way.

She lifted the receiver and asked quietly, 'Who is
it?'

'What do you think you're doing?' Jake asked, and his voice was filled with anger.

Two jealous men, she thought wryly. She felt like the bone between two savage dogs, but of the two Jake was easier to cope with; he did not frighten her and James did. She was not sure of James. There was a brooding darkness in him which frightened her, drew her and frightened her at one and the same time.

'I can't discuss it over the telephone,' she said, aware of James's listening presence.

He stalked to the door and went out, slamming it behind him. Caroline sighed.

'Jake, I realise it must seem inexplicable to you, but I'll explain as best as I can when I see you.'

'Just one question, sweetie,' Jake said unpleasantly. 'Did you spend the night with him?'

At that point she knew that how she answered would decide everything, and in the seconds before she spoke whole centuries of time seemed to pass. She had never had the ability to think quickly, but she thought then, with terrible clarity.

'Yes,' she said at last.

Jake slammed the phone down.

She could have told him the whole truth then. She could have taken her time to decide. It was what she had intended to do. She still did not know for certain which of the men she preferred, but something in her nature turned finally towards the dark uncertainties of James's character, partly because she knew in her heart of hearts which of them needed her, wanted her most.

She slipped on a comfortable dressing-gown. She had had it for years, the warm beige angora material worn with age. Her 'bunny coat', James had called it, and although she had sexier, more flattering wraps to wear, she still found it comforting to slip into at times.

James was in the kitchen, the flower-splashed blinds up to reveal the wind-torn, rain-swept garden. He was watching the coffee hit the percolator dome, his face harsh.

He glanced round as she entered the room, his eyes shuttered. 'I've checked the supplies ... there are eggs but no bacon, but plenty of bread.'

'Boiled eggs, then?' she asked calmly.

'If you like.'

She set out the twin eggcups with their gaudy yellow buttercup frivolity, the matching napkins and woven straw table-mats.

James watched her as she moved about, her dressing-gown floating around her slim figure. 'What did Redway say?' he asked at last, in a carefully cool tone.

'Not much,' she said, dropping the eggs into the boiling water.

'Jealous, was he?' James sounded malicious, a sneer in his voice.

She glanced at him and he flushed, looking away.

'He didn't like it much,' she admitted.

'But you told him nothing happened,' he said, then, savagely, 'By the skin of your teeth!'

'One egg or two?' she asked.

'One,' he said with his mouth turning down.

Over the meal she asked conversationally, 'Where shall we buy a place in London? Any favourite district?'

'Several,' he said, looking up. 'We're still going

ahead, then? You are staying with me?'

'I thought I'd made that clear,' she said.

'Not very.' He broke off a piece of toast and played with it, head bent. 'Why, Caro?'

'We're married,' she said.

'You were planning to divorce me.'

'When I thought you cared for someone else,' she explained.

'Was that the only reason?' He stared at her, brows together.

'Oh, yes,' she said calmly. 'I'm like you in that, James. I won't share with anyone.'

The silvery eyes narrowed suddenly. 'Who did you think I was seeing? You must have given this other woman a name?' His curiosity had awoken suddenly and she felt instinctively that it would be better not to satisfy it. She inwardly grimaced at herself, knowing that she did not want James to be made aware of Linda Blare, to think of her in that connection.

'No,' she said, eyes steady. 'I just felt that your withdrawal had to have a cause.'

'So you jumped to the conclusion that it was another woman?'

'It seemed logical.'

He stared at the rainwashed window, his features taut. 'I wish to God it had been!'

'I don't,' she said teasingly, and his eyes came back to her, a brightness in them.

'No?' His mouth curved into a smile. 'Maybe not. I'm glad about that, anyway.' A sigh wrenched at him, brooding on his hard mouth. 'Jealousy is hell, isn't it?'

'Hell,' she agreed, watching him. There had to be

some reason for his morbid jealousy, for the depth and coldness of it. She was only now becoming aware of how little she knew him, how rarely they had talked with any degree of honesty about their lives. James had shut her up whenever she began to talk of her life before she met him, and she saw now that his jealousy had been the root of that. Somehow he had been as silent on the subject of his own life before meeting her, and now she wondered if they might not need to talk about it. Exposing the roots of his jealousy might kill it.

The rain stopped during the morning and they drove through the Kent countryside to have lunch at a pub beside the sea. The familiar landscape moved past as they made their way down the motorway, the hop fields, the crooked lines of oasthouses white on the sky like monks' cowls, the rich green meadows and little clumps of trees clustered around ponds in which cows drank, belly-deep. They had often spent a Sunday in this way during the first year of their marriage, and they made their way to a favourite pub by instinct.

Afterwards, sitting in the pub garden, watching some children playing on swings nearby, Caroline asked him, 'What sort of childhood did you have, James?'

He gave her a shrewd, amused look, and she knew he read her mind. 'Trying to find reasons, darling? Playing at psychiatrist? Don't bother. I had a very well-ordered childhood, very English, with a nanny and a prep school followed by public school.'

'And your parents?' She would not let him mock her into giving up her probing. Something had to have made him the way he was, and she meant to find out.

'Were quiet, well-bred English parents,' he said. 'They did their very best for me. I was an only child, remember. I lacked nothing.'

'Lots of love?' she asked softly.

He grinned. 'My parents weren't the sort to be demonstrative, but I never doubted that they cared for me. Boys don't like demonstrative parents, remember . . . it embarrasses them.'

She watched him, frowning. Somewhere there had to be a key which would unlock the complexities of that dark mind of his.

As if he had read her mind again, he said soberly, 'It's a kink in my nature, Caroline. Why do you think I tried so hard to hide it from you? I hate the way I feel, but I can't do a thing about it.'

'Perhaps having it out into the open will make a difference,' she said.

'Perhaps,' he muttered. He gave her a brief look. 'Are you going to go on with this TV series?'

'Yes,' she said, meeting his eyes levelly.

He nodded, glancing away.

'Having a job will make all the difference to me,' she explained.

'Yes,' he said, but his voice was rough.

'Say what you're thinking, James,' she said gently. 'Say it.'

'I don't want you seeing Redway day after day,' he burst out, and she quickly put a hand over one of his, shaking her head at him.

'James, if you seriously think that keeping me away from Jake will alter the way I feel you're blind ... emotions aren't altered by circumstances. If I loved Jake I would go on loving him even if I never saw him.'

He lifted her hand to his mouth, kissing it hungrily. 'You don't love him?'

'I love you,' she said, her eyes on his face. 'Didn't the fact that I'm staying tell you that?'

'God, I wanted to believe it,' he muttered. 'But there seemed some doubt in your mind.'

'There was,' she admitted. 'Not any more ... I chose, last night, and I chose for good.'

They went home through a gathering English dusk, the sky fading in soft rose colours shot with grey, the birds noisy with that special evening lyricism which heralds the approach of night. When they drew up outside the house they saw Jake's car outside. James shot Caroline a guarded look, his grey eyes blank.

'Redway,' he said through tight lips.

'Yes,' she said, feeling nervous and strung up. What was Jake doing here? Somehow she had anticipated that he would not make a move. His long silence during her marriage had convinced her that Jake could walk away from her without a backward glance.

They got out and Jake came out of his car, a cigarette in his hand. He strolled towards them gracefully, a broad, lazy figure, maddeningly in command of himself.

James put a hand on her elbow, the lightest touch, yet she felt the anger in him as though it burned her.

'Hallo, angel,' Jake drawled. He was acting and

she knew it. He only used that artificial voice when
he was putting on a show.

'Jake,' she said, smiling, and her smile was as unreal as his expression.

A look flashed between them, brief as lightning
and as searing. James had not relinquished his hold
on her. He was staring at Jake expressionlessly. It
surprised Caroline to realise that he had slightly
more height, his dark head an inch or two above
Jake's charmingly untidy one.

Jake transferred his eyes to James's face. 'I
thought,' he said, 'that it was time your husband and
I had a more civilised encounter.' He held out his
hand, his face mocking. 'Mr Advocate.'

James slowly took the hand, nodding. 'Redway.'

The words were uttered politely, but they might
as well have snarled at each other. The effect was
the same.

Their hands dropped away. Jake gave Caroline
another of his meaningless smiles. 'Aren't you going
to offer me a drink, Caro?'

'Of course,' she said, smiling back, her facial
muscles aching from the strain.

James opened the door and switched on the hall
light. Jake stood back while Caroline walked inside,
then he followed her. James walked to the drink
cabinet and asked curtly, 'Sherry?'

'Whisky if you have it,' Jake murmured.

James got out the glasses, poured him a drink,
handed it to him with a look which barely touched
his face, then poured himself another. Caroline's
heart sank as she saw how much he was pouring. He
swallowed it rapidly, his fingers clenched around
the glass.

Jake was watching him shrewdly, eyes narrowed, and he was merely sipping his whisky. Caroline stood there, not knowing what to say.

Jake turned towards her, malice in his eyes. 'I came to find out if you're still doing the series, Caroline. Paddy will need to be sure he can rely on you.'

'Yes,' she said, 'I'm still doing it.'

Jake glanced at James with a lifted brow. 'Sure about that?'

James finished his drink and poured himself another, offering the decanter to Jake, who shook his head with a look of curiosity in his eyes.

'I'm quite certain,' Caroline said, willing Jake to go.

'Good,' he said softly. 'I'm looking forward to working with you again, Caro. We have some interesting scenes together.' While he spoke his eyes were on James's back and both he and Caroline saw the contraction of James's muscles at the words.

James turned and walked out of the elegant room without a glance or a word to either of them, and Jake whistled under his breath.

'I see just what Maggie meant about him ... icy, isn't he?'

'You'd better go,' Caroline said with a sigh.

'Not on your life, darling,' said Jake, and there was angry determination in the look he gave her. 'This time that husband of yours isn't freezing me out.' He put down his glass and moved towards her and she took a step backwards.

'Don't back away,' Jake said. 'I want the truth and I want it now, Caro. Why did you go back to him so suddenly last night; why out of the blue like that?' His eyes held hers fiercely. 'You know very well it was a very odd time to choose.'

She felt her colour deepening and her eyes shifted. 'He's my husband.'

'That didn't seem to make much difference earlier in the evening,' he said, and the swift blow made her draw a shaky breath.

'Jake, don't!'

'Don't what? Remind you that I know you wanted me as much as I wanted you last night? Why not? You got frightened, did you? Ran back to him?'

'I did some thinking,' she said faintly.

'God, women should be banned from it!' he muttered. 'And what did you have to think about?'

'Options,' she said with a wry smile.

'Such as?'

She met his eyes with a pretence of calm. 'Jake, if you never saw me again after today, how much would it matter?'

His face hardened. 'A hell of a lot ... how can you even ask? You mean more to me than I've ever told you.'

'Because of our years at drama school?'

'That among other things,' he said, his eyes on her face. 'I've always fancied you, Caro.'

She smiled ruefully. 'Fancied me, yes ... but would it be the end of everything if you never saw me again?'

He stared at her in silence for a moment. 'Are you telling me that it would be for him?'

She felt a smile touching her mouth, involuntary,

affectionate. 'You always could leap two steps ahead of me, Jake. Yes, that's what I'm telling you. James loves me.'

'I don't?' The question was terse, sharp.

'Not that badly,' she said.

He turned away and walked to the window. With his back to her he said, 'And does what you feel come into this at any point, Caro?'

Last night she had told herself she would choose according to her own needs, but in the end she had chosen differently, and she knew it.

'Yes,' she said gently.

Jake was silent for a moment, then he asked, 'What about the other woman? You said he had one.'

'I was mistaken. There was only me.'

Jake swung and looked at her. 'Let me get this straight ... you left him because there was someone else, and you went back because there wasn't?'

His questions were going too close to the heart of it and she looked away. 'We're starting again,' she told him. 'Trying to make our marriage work.'

'And me?' He watched her, eyes probing.

'Last night was a wrong turning,' she said, not quite meeting his stare. 'I was miserable and lonely and you offered me comfort.'

'So thanks and goodbye?' His voice stung.

'I'm sorry, Jake.'

He turned his head as James came back into the room. She watched the two men assess each other with cold eyes.

'I'm going, Fox,' Jake said tauntingly. 'Goodnight, Caro. I'll look forward to seeing you again soon. Paddy will be in touch with rehearsal dates.'

He walked out and the front door slammed. James studied her with cool, expressionless eyes. 'You look tired. An early night would be a good idea. I have work to do, so I'll stay down here for a while.'

She nodded, kissed his cheek and went up to bed. Only as she fell asleep did it occur to her distantly that James had withdrawn again into his work, that things had barely changed at all.

She woke early and had time to think, lying there, listening to James's quiet breathing. He lay on his side, his back to her, and she knew that it was deliberate. She closed her eyes, sliding smoothly over the sheet, cuddling up to his back, pretending to sleep. After a while he moved, but it was to get out of the bed. She kept her eyes closed and heard him go to the bathroom, heard the distant sound of the shower, then after a while his footsteps on the stairs.

Slipping into her only really sexy nightwear, a black lace negligee which she had worn on her honeymoon and rarely since, Caroline pattered down the stairs and found him moving around the kitchen making his breakfast.

'Sorry I overslept,' she said brightly.

He shot her a look which widened as he took in what she wore, then he turned back to the toast he was making. 'It doesn't matter.'

She came over to him, her negligee floating, and leaned against him, kissing his averted cheek. 'Mmm ... your skin is cold. That's the aftershave I bought you on your birthday, isn't it?'

'Yes,' he said, and as he turned to look at her she stood on tiptoe and kissed his mouth lightly. 'Smells nice,' she said.

His arm came round her then and his lips came down hard, seeking response hungrily. She wound her arms round his neck and kissed him back, her fingers moving in his dark hair. She felt the flame leap up in him. His body betrayed it, shuddering against her, but he drew back slowly and turned towards the coffee pot. 'Want some coffee?'

It was not going to be easy, she thought. Old habits die hard and James had twice as much pride as any normal man. He was fighting her hard, struggling to maintain his self-control, trying even now to hide the way he felt from her. Once she would have shrunk away from the cold front he was showing her, but now she was going to thaw it even if it took a lifetime.

When he had gone to work she dressed and went shopping in the village, meeting curious eyes with a bland smile and a few prepared words. 'A holiday, yes ... oh, a lovely time, thank you.'

'You look better,' Jean Eddows, the doctor's wife, told her with approval. 'I was worried about you for a long time. A break has done you good. You're a different girl.'

'I feel it,' Caroline said, smiling.

'Come to dinner,' Jean invited impulsively, and Caroline said with a smile, 'Love to!'

They consulted diaries and made an arrangement. 'James will be free,' Caroline promised, and made a mental note to insist that he was.

Mrs Carter was amazed to see her. 'I didn't know

you were back, Mrs Fox. Mr Fox didn't say anything.'

Caroline assumed the calm smile she had prac-
tised in the village. 'I surprised him,' she said. 'He
was missing me, although he would never admit it.'

'Men all over,' smiled Mrs Carter, nodding. 'My
husband's the same ... stubborn as a mule, but that
helpless!'

James arrived earlier than she had expected and
she saw his car from the bedroom as she stood in her
slip choosing a dress. He came into the house and
she heard him standing there, listening to the
silence. As if she had been able to see him she knew
what he was thinking. He did not call her name,
only walked from room to room, then came up the
stairs, very slowly. For a moment he stood on the
landing, then he pushed open the bedroom door
and Caroline looked across the room at him.

For a second before the mask flashed down into
place she saw the grey agony of his face. He had not
expected to see her. He had thought she had gone.

'Darling, you're early,' she said lightly, coming towards him in her black lace slip.

He almost backed; she could feel the instinctive
reflex reaction in her bones. Then she slid her arms
round his neck and his head came down abruptly,
his mouth clamping over her own, his hands reaching out for her.

She arched under the possessive caress of his
hands, beginning to breathe quickly, curving in to
him with her fingers in his hair and her head
thrown back under the fierce hunger of his mouth.

He lifted her into his arms easily, still kissing her,
and carried her to the bed. Last time she had fought

him desperately, resisting with every muscle, but now she was provoking, inciting, her hands running over him as their mouths explored each other hotly, and when he pressed her down with the full weight of his body she submitted with eagerness.

Neither of them had spoken a word. Their love-making had a silent desperation which she found painful. James was hurting her, but she made no protest, giving him what he wanted without holding back, and when the wild, sweet feeling swept her away with him the sounds which broke from her seemed to startle him, as though he had barely been conscious of anything but the satisfying of his own need. He lifted his dark head and looked at her briefly before burying it again against her body, his lips hot.

They lay on the bed, heavy with satisfaction, and Caroline slipped into a sleep which was dreamless and engulfing. When she woke the room was dark and James was holding her in the circle of his arms.

She stirred and his head moved to look down at her. There was a smile on his mouth.

'You slept like a baby,' he said slightly teasingly.

'Did you?'

'No,' he said. 'I just watched you.'

She laughed, stretching, and felt his hand tighten, as though merely the movement of her body against him could flick passion into life in him. 'I'm not sure I like that,' she said.

'Why not?' A frown touched his forehead.

'Sleep makes one vulnerable,' she said, and then remembered his telling her that she had once spoken Jake's name in her sleep. He was remembering too, she knew it by the icy formality on his face.

She was beginning to read those expressions of his now that she knew the key to them.

She stretched again, deliberately, her hand moving up his bare chest, the fingers curling into his dark body hair. 'I was dreaming,' she said, winding a hair round her little finger and tugging it.

'Oh?' He sounded remote.

'I dreamt you made love to me,' she lied without caring that she was lying. 'I can't think why.'

She felt his body relax. 'Can't you?' He began to smile, his grey eyes dancing. 'Wish fulfilment? Glad to oblige any time, my darling.' His hands moved pleasurably, his mouth brushed her bare shoulder. 'Caro,' he muttered against her warm skin. 'Caro.'

If it took for ever, she thought, lifting her head to meet his mouth, she would make him trust her, make him come out of that cold shell of his.

At the back of her head a little voice asked warningly if she could take this endless effort to soothe his jealousy, but she brushed it away.

'Aren't you hungry?' she asked him some time later, and he groaned, 'Yes, desperately,' but he wasn't talking about food and she laughed at him.

'I had planned a special dinner.'

'If you insist,' he said reluctantly. 'I could think of better ways of passing the evening.'

'What there is left of it,' she said ruefully, looking at the clock. 'I must have needed that sleep.'

'I needed you,' he said, and she leapt off the bed, graceful, aware of his eyes. She slid into a negligee, tied it at the waist and made a face at him. 'If you aren't hungry I am!'

Over the meal James asked, 'What did you do today?'

'Not much,' she said. 'Shopped. Oh, I met Jean . . .
she asked us to dinner on Thursday, and I said we
would go. You'll come home in time, won't you?'

'If I must,' he groaned.

'You must . . . it's ages since we had a meal with
them. It will be fun, and now I've promised we must
go.'

'I suppose I can stand it,' he said without en-
thusiasm. Then he poured himself another cup of
coffee and asked, 'Thought any more about selling
this house?'

'Yes,' she said firmly. 'I'll get an estate agent to
come and value it for us, shall I?'

'If you like,' he said, looking away, his tone expressionless.

She watched the dark profile. 'We'll see much
more of each other,' she pointed out. 'You won't
have this long journey to and from work and we'll
have more free time together.'

'London isn't my idea of a place to live,' he said.
'Working there is bad enough, and when I'm on circuit I shan't be seeing much of you, anyway.'

She was silent, her head bent. After a moment
James said brusquely, 'But if that's what you
want . . .'

She lifted her head. 'It is,' she said.

He nodded, the grey eyes bleak. 'Just as you wish.'

But Caroline felt her heart contract uneasily
under the cold look of his eyes and again she asked
herself how long she would be able to stand the
whip of his jealous need to isolate her from everyone but himself.

CHAPTER EIGHT

THEY dined with Jean and Bob Eddows, as they had arranged, and the evening turned out to be a very pleasant one. James could be charming when he unbent and Jean was fluttering volubly as she sat next to him, responsive to the smile in his grey eyes. Caroline watched him secretly, tracing the hard, austere bone structure, the arched black brows which could with so slight a movement convey contempt, rage, coldness, the shape and depth of those grey eyes, the long Roman nose, and beneath it the line of his mouth, relaxed at the moment, smiling, but which could turn savage in a second, could hurt and elate when he kissed her.

Bob took him off to see the new billiard table he had installed in the cellar of his Victorian house and Jean watched them go with an ecstatic sigh. 'Quite a man, your husband.'

'Thank you,' Caroline said lightly, smiling at her. 'So is yours.'

Jean made a loving face. 'Oh, Bob's a darling and I love him dearly, but let's face it, Caroline ... James is pure wish fulfilment! Every woman likes to dream occasionally and that man of yours is dream-material ... what does he look like in his wig and gown? Sexy, I bet.'

No, Caroline thought. In court James looked dangerous; a cold-eyed, ruthless opponent, his features carved of stone, his tongue cruel as he lashed his victims. She would not like to face him in the dock. It was bad enough when that mood came on him at home.

He still frightened her and she knew it. She felt utterly inadequate faced with the steely plating of his personality. Flashes of bitter hostility still radiated from him now and then and she found herself coming close to losing her temper violently under the bite of his tongue. It took all her self-control to hold back the retorts which rose to her mind.

They were existing in a limbo, acting politely, being very careful with each other, but when the telephone rang she saw his eyes narrow on her in immediate suspicion, and as she picked up the post each day she was aware of his watchful gaze. He had not dismissed Jake from his mind and he was sure that neither had she, although there was total silence from Jake and she was sure he was amusing himself more than adequately elsewhere. Jake would not be eating his heart out for her.

When James told her that he had to go to Leicester for a week to conduct the defence in a big trial, she held her expression steady, because she was very aware of the watchful coldness of his eyes.

'You'll be all right?'

'Yes,' she said carefully, 'of course.'

During his absence she went up to London to see Maggie. She had put off that interview because she had not looked forward to it, and when Maggie opened the door of the flat she gave her an angry look. Ruefully, Caroline held out her hands. 'Oh, come in,' Maggie said grimly, stepping aside without taking them, but it was not in her nature to bear a grudge. Her old affection for Caroline crept through her sulky expression after a few moments.

'Why?' she asked, though. 'Caro, why in God's name did you do it?'

'He's my husband,' Caroline said.

'He nearly drove you insane before,' Maggie snapped. 'Have you gone back to let him finish the job?'

It might yet come to that, Caroline thought, but she said aloud, 'Poor James, you really have it in for him, don't you?'

Maggie was unabashed, as partisan as ever, and her face was stubborn as she asked, 'What about Jake?'

'Jake will survive,' Caroline said with a gleam of humour. 'He's pretty good at bouncing, Maggie.'

Maggie looked vital, her golden eyes brilliant. 'Caro, don't you know Jake ...'

Caroline could not let her say that. Quickly she said, 'I know Jake as well as you do, Maggie, and I know he'll be fine.'

'You're crazy,' Maggie said fiercely. 'James Fox is a cold, arrogant bastard and you know it.'

'I love him,' Caroline shrugged.

'Oh, Caro, sometimes you make me so mad!'

Caroline laughed. 'I'm sorry, Maggie. I knew the score when I went back to him. I know what I'm getting. James isn't an easy man to live with ... but he's a damned sight harder to live without. I could walk out on him now, but in no time at all I'd be back on my knees to him, because I know perfectly well that I can't live without him.'

Maggie had to believe the final ring of her voice,

but she clearly found it maddening, incomprehensible. 'You're a fool,' she told her. 'Jake's worth ten of him.'

Caroline looked away and changed the subject. She would not let Maggie talk to her of Jake; they could never see eye to eye on that subject. But Maggie had not abandoned her efforts to get them together, because at some time during the morning, while Caroline was out of the room, she must have called him. He arrived just as they were going off to eat lunch, and from Maggie's self-conscious face Caroline knew perfectly well he had been summoned.

She gave no sign of being aware of it, though. 'Hallo, Jake,' she said calmly.

He looked at her with mocking, narrowed eyes. 'Caro,' he said, nodding. 'Fancy seeing you.'

He came to lunch with them and a stranger might have been excused for missing the undercurrents because all three of them were acting like mad, talking lightly, cheerfully.

'Drop me and take Caro to the station to catch her train,' Maggie said afterwards, and Jake nodded.

He did not, however, drive to the station. He took the road over one of London's bridges, the sky blue and cloudless on either side of them as they drove over the river. Looking down over the wide, bending water, Caroline asked warily, 'Where are you taking me, Jake?'

'Home,' he said.

'Don't be absurd. I can get the train.'

'I feel like a country drive,' he retorted, staring ahead. 'James is away, you said. You can't be in any hurry to get back.'

'It isn't a good idea,' she said nervously.

He didn't answer, merely driving on, and she did not feel like a long argument with him, so she sat back and said nothing else.

'How are things going?' he asked as they passed through the long, ugly ribbon of suburban London.

'Fine,' she lied.

He shot her a wry look. 'Try that again, darling, and with more conviction this time. Surely you can act better than that, Caro.'

'Beast,' she said, laughing, because Jake had always made her laugh, he had such a comical face under those rough eyebrows.

'Is he jealous of me?' Jake asked, and she drew a sharp breath.

He looked at her again, his eyes shrewd. 'Sick with it, is he? I noticed it when I dropped in to see you the other day. He doesn't like the idea of you doing that series, does he?'

'No,' she said.

'He'll like it a lot less when he gets a look at the scripts,' Jake said mischievously, cocking a teasing eye at her.

'Why?' she asked anxiously.

'One of the love scenes burns the paper it's written on,' he said cheerfully.

'Oh, dear,' she muttered to herself.

'I'm looking forward to it,' said Jake, grinning.

Caroline gave him a furious glare.

'Maggie has a theory about him,' Jake told her. 'She reckons he feels it was beneath his dignity to marry an actress and he's tried to cut you off from us all to bury the memory.'

Caroline had heard Maggie on the subject of

James, and she did not want to hear any more of her theories. 'She doesn't know James,' she said.

'He's frightened of me, isn't he?' Jake asked casually.

She tensed. 'What makes you say that?'

'I've got eyes, my love. He would have chucked me out when I came on Sunday, but he was afraid you might go with me, so he tried to behave like a perfect gentleman, and the effort was too much for him. He walked out to stop himself throttling me.'

Jake had always been a shrewd judge of character, and they had often played a game of guessing the sort of people they were passing in the street. It had been part of their method of studying acting. Caroline was anxious, looking at him with worried eyes. 'Jake, my marriage matters to me ... don't undermine it.'

'How could I do that, darling?' he asked in mock surprise, but the glint in his eyes told her that he knew perfectly well what he could do if he tried, and she did not trust him.

When they arrived at the house he followed her inside and she felt vulnerable, facing him. 'Would you like a drink?' she asked for something to occupy her hands.

'Whisky,' he said, and she poured him a glass, taking it to him.

He lay back casually in a graceful posture along the couch, his arm stretched out, the glass in one hand. 'Sit down,' he said, patting the place beside him, and, when she hesitated, 'I won't bite you, Caro.' As she gingerly sat down he added mockingly, 'Although the idea is tempting.'

Deliberately she asked him a question about the

TV series and he plunged into a lengthy conversation, telling her the details of the location work he expected, grimacing over the man they had got to play Wellington.

'He's reliable,' she protested.

'Wood from the neck up,' Jake shrugged.

She got him another drink and he watched her walk across the room towards him, his eyes flicking from her long legs to the blaze of her hair.

She was nervous under that probing gaze. 'You'd better not drink too much,' she said. 'You have that drive back to London.'

He watched her through his lashes. 'I could always beg a bed here, couldn't I?'

She flushed. 'No, Jake.'

His hand moved, smoothing down the skin of her forearm. 'No?'

For one moment they stared at each other in silence. 'No,' she repeated flatly. She had made a mistake when she let him see that she feared his intervention in her marriage. Jake did not need to be told twice.

He swallowed his whisky. 'Aren't you even going to feed me?' He sounded plaintive. 'The best I'll get on the road back is egg and chips at a roadside café.'

Faced with the question she could hardly refuse. She went into the kitchen and made him an omelette stuffed with mushrooms and onion. He grinned over it. 'Quite the little housewife now.' He surveyed her. 'What a waste, though.'

He did not go for several hours and she was on tenterhooks all the time, the worst part of it being that Jake knew; his lazy, mocking eyes informed her that he knew. He was teasing her deliberately and she could not face him with it without bringing out into the open things her mind warned her should stay hidden.

She walked with him to the door and he halted, leaning his back against it, eyeing her curiously. 'It isn't a crime, you know,' he said softly.

'What?' she asked flushing.

He put a hand under her chin, his fingers stroking her cheek. 'To fancy someone,' he said, looking into her eyes.

Her colour deepened. 'Goodnight, Jake.'

'Let me stay,' he whispered.

Her pose deserted her. 'No!' she said angrily.

'Caro, you can't hide it from me, any more than you can from him ... any more than I can from you.' He smiled at her caressingly. 'You're very lovely, darling, and I've waited a long time for you.'

'I love him,' she said in a husky voice, because she could not make herself unaware of the temptation of Jake's caressing hands and voice. 'James means more to me than anyone in the world.'

His hands fell away. He turned and went without a word, banging the door, and Caroline went to bed feeling as though she had been hanging on a cliff edge with a long, long drop below her.

James came back a day earlier than he had intended and without warning, so that she was already in bed when she heard his car and then the quiet closing of the front door. She stumbled out of bed and pulled on a wrap, sleepily blinking as he opened the bedroom door and looked at her.

'You're early,' she said, coming to kiss him, and

his arm held her for a moment before he looked down at her with a faint smile.

'Poor darling, did I wake you?'

'It doesn't matter ... can I cook you something?'

'I have eaten,' he said. 'I'll get a drink, though, then I'll come to bed.'

She got back into bed and waited for him. A few moments later he came into the room carrying a glass. 'Did the trial go well?' she asked.

He nodded, his back to her, taking off his jacket and tie. She watched him carefully hanging up his clothes and felt the usual quiver of sexual excitement at the lean, hard body as he walked across the room. He swallowed some of his whisky. 'How did you amuse yourself while I was away?' he asked.

She had to tell him. 'I had lunch with Maggie,' she said lightly, watching the cold structure of his face.

'Just Maggie?' he asked expressionlessly.

Caroline hesitated, and that was a mistake. He gave her a brief, chill glance. 'Redway too,' he said for her, flatly.

She licked her lips nervously. 'Yes,' she said, wishing to God she had said it the first time, because she knew that hard mask, and she was shivering as though the Ice Age had come again.

'Which train did you catch back?' he asked, and she met the probe of his stare unhappily.

'Jake drove me back.'

'Kind of him,' he said, the words falling icily. 'I hope he liked my whisky.'

She started and knew that he had already guessed before he came up here. She looked at his whisky glass and closed her eyes in misery.

'Did he drink it before or afterwards?' James asked, and the tone left no doubt as to his meaning.

'Don't, James,' she begged in anguish.

'I'm sure you made him welcome,' he said tightly.

'For God's sake, James!'

He put the glass down with a crash. 'In my own house? Was it this bed, you little bitch?'

Caroline sprang out of bed, shaking. 'No, James, it isn't true!'

He caught her before she got to the door, his hands so violent that she cried out in pain. 'I didn't, James ... believe me!'

'Do you take me for a fool? You weren't going to tell me, were you? I had to drag it out of you. He was here, drinking my whisky, enjoying my wife ...'

'No!'

'Every time you see him you have it written all over you,' James muttered hoarsely. 'Anyone seeing you together would know ... it stands out like neon lighting.'

She looked at him in horror, because it was true, and she knew it. At Simone's party, she had been deeply aware of it. Yet how could she ever get James to believe that the physical magnetism which drew her to Jake had no bearing on the love she felt for him? Why should one assume that a woman is incapable of sexual attraction unless she is deeply in love? she asked herself. Jake is a sexy man and I'm very fond of him. The two emotions are unconnected. I was fond of him long before I felt the tug of his attraction. I will go on being fond of him. The way I love James isn't touched by either thing.

James was staring at her, reading guilt in her flushed, worried face. She whispered huskily,

'James, I've never slept with Jake, I swear it!'

'Don't lie to me!' he shouted, and the ice of his manner cracked, revealing the barbaric jealousy beneath. His hands closed roughly over her shoulders. He looked down at the black lace of her nightdress, his grey eyes scorching the white skin of her shoulders, the long bare throat and the half-revealed breasts. 'Did you enjoy it, Caroline? How does he make love?'

'Don't,' she breathed, lips trembling.

'Like this?' He dragged her against his body, his mouth bruising her lips in naked ferocity, using the maximum of force, as though he needed to hurt, forcing back her head until her stretched neck ached. When he lifted his head at last his eyes glittered. 'Or is he more persuasive, my darling? What sort of lover is he?'

Temper and humiliation made her reckless. 'He wouldn't maul me about, anyway,' she flung back.

The grey eyes flashed. 'Wouldn't he?' He lowered his head and his mouth moved over her exposed throat, sliding down her skin, his lips moist and warm. 'Is that more like it?' he asked, brushing her shoulders with his lips, his hands moving up to her breasts.

'James ...' She was trembling, aroused by the caressing movements.

He looked at her then with an emotion so close to hatred that she flinched under it. 'You little bitch!' he breathed. 'One week and you're back in bed with him.'

'Why won't you listen? James, it isn't true!'

His hand hit her across the face and she was knocked off balance, falling across the bed. He was beside her before she had recovered, his hands brutal as they ripped the nightdress away, then his mouth closed over her breast and she pushed at his black head, vainly trying to fight him. His hands moved, shaping her body, following the soft warm curve from breast to thigh, and she began to feel the slow, inexorable rise of desire inside herself.

She arched, gasping, and her hands fell from his dark hair to the lean back, her nails raking his skin, feeling the muscles beneath her fingers flex. The hoarse rasp of his breathing increased.

She could not let him take her in this mood. 'I love you, James,' she told him, clinging to him. 'I love you.'

'You're lying,' he muttered. 'But I don't give a damn ... Oh, God, I want you. You drive me mad.'

The darkness in him engulfed her and she wound her arms around his back, kissing his throat, arching responsively beneath the driving body.

Sweat glistened on his pale temples and dewed his back. His hands bruised and explored, their touch rough. He was taking her ruthlessly, without tenderness, but her anxiety and anger was being released into a wild, frenzied response which seemed to incite him into more and more brutal lovemaking. She knew suddenly that she needed it, that some deeply buried instinct was making her not merely accept but want the savagery of his body.

After the acute agonising tension was released, they lay together like spent runners, panting. James's skin was burning under her cheek. He lay there for a while, trying to get his breath back, then he moved and switched on the bedside lamp and looked at her with a white face. 'How much did I hurt you?' he asked her wearily. The grey eyes skimmed over her and she saw him wince. 'Oh, God, those bruises ... what the hell have I done to you?'

'It doesn't matter,' she said quickly. She tried to smile. 'You are a brutal lover, that's all, James.'

He flinched at that. 'This can't go on,' he muttered. 'I've no right to inflict this on you.'

'I love you,' she said gently. 'James, I wasn't lying about Jake ... he never laid a hand on me.'

He nodded in that weary, self-sickened way. 'I'm sorry. Of course I believe you. I went out of my mind.' He looked at her body with agonised eyes. 'I've hurt you this time, really hurt you—don't pretend I haven't. When I knew you'd seen Redway I wanted to kill you. I stood downstairs looking at the whisky and I had these visions flashing round my brain ... of you in his arms ... it drove me frantic.'

'Forget it,' she said softly, stroking his cheek.

'Don't you understand? One day I might kill you ... I nearly did tonight.'

'You made love to me instead,' she said, smiling at him.

'And left these bruises?' His eyes flashed to her marked body with shame and self-contempt. 'Do you think I'm complacent about having done this to you?'

'I forgive you,' she said seriously.

'I don't forgive myself,' he said, biting out the words. 'Caro, I've got to go away. I must come to terms with this, fight it somehow. I can't do that with you around. I've got to think clearly, and near you I can't think at all.'

Was that the problem? she wondered. How did the clever brain inside James's handsome head coexist with the brutal, passionate instincts of his body? Was there war between the two? Was he divided, torn between the two halves of his nature? Did he find that the icy cleverness of his mind failed when his body was in control? Did his wits desert him faced with an emotional problem such as theirs? He had been carefully educated to use his mind. Cool, strong intelligence, however, could not solve problems raised by the emotional turmoil of the body.

'All you have to think is that I'm telling you the truth,' she insisted. 'I love you, James, just as you are ... I won't deny you hurt me tonight, and I won't deny that I enjoyed it.'

He looked taken aback and she laughed wryly. 'You think I shouldn't? Perhaps you're right. But I did. Perhaps that's why I want you, not Jake, my darling. Something in me responds to the darkness in you.'

He stared at her, brows drawn together. 'Are you just saying that? Trying to be kind? I don't want your kindness, Caro.'

'And I don't want your pride,' she said fiercely. 'I want the truth between us.'

'I wonder if you even know what that is,' he said. 'How close were you to Redway, Caro, all those years ago?'

She watched him carefully, her face tense. 'Very,' she said.

'You were a virgin when we married,' he said, as if to himself. 'That surprised me.'

'Thanks,' she said tartly.

'I suspected he'd been your lover then.'

'He wasn't.'

'I knew that later,' he admitted. 'But he would have been, I think.'

Their eyes met and she sighed. 'Oh, perhaps.' There was no point in lying. He must know it.

'And if he had his way he would be now.'

'Perhaps,' she admitted in a low voice.

'We know where Redway and I stand ... where do you?' He met her eyes and held up a hand to stop her speaking. 'No, wait a moment ... I'm leaving you, Caroline.'

She blenched. 'James! I've told you ...'

'Listen,' he said. 'I can't bear to go on hurting you like this. I'm afraid one day it will go too far. I'll go too far. I'm not in command of myself where you're concerned. While my mind is working clearly, let me put this to you ... I want a separation.'

'No,' she protested. 'No, James!'

'You can have an allowance,' he said. 'Get a flat.' His mouth twisted. 'Or share one.' And she knew who was in his mind. 'Give us both time to sort things out.'

She stared at him, angry that he could even suggest it. 'And if I see Jake?'

He looked at her grimly. 'That's for you to decide. I'm setting you free, Caro. No man has the right to hurt another human being the way I'm hurting you. We both have to think about what the future holds. I have to fight this thing somehow, and I'll never do it near you.'

He would not listen to argument. His mind was made up, and all her pleading, argument, coaxing, failed.

A week later she was installed in Maggie's flat as a paying guest. Maggie was elated and Jake, when he heard of it, gave Caroline a long, probing glance. 'Am I permitted to cheer?' he asked drily, and she shook her head at him without a smile.

The rehearsals for the TV series began a week later. Caroline's scenes with Jake were being shot in the studio. Most of the filming was being done on location in Spain, but it was cheaper to shoot the rest on the lot.

Caroline was shaken by her costumes. Jake eyed them with raised eyebrows, whistling. 'Sexy,' he murmured.

They were wildly revealing, she thought glumly, looking at herself in the mirror. Empire-style, bound with wide sashes of silk under her high breasts, they revealed a good deal, their fine muslin clinging to her body like a second skin.

She found the technique of acting for the small screen greatly different from the techniques she had learnt in the theatre, but Jake had already prepared her for a playing-down of emotion, a voice control, a use of the minimum of movement.

'Not so much gesture,' Paddy shouted at her now and then, and she strove to keep her hands still, willing her body to obey her brain. It was hard to break habits learnt over years.

The scene she dreaded most was the one where she went to bed with Jake. Everyone treated the scene like any other, however, and she began to relax after a while. Jake, however, was in a teasing mood, his eyes mocking. Paddy picked him up. 'This isn't comedy, Jake. Take it again, and wipe the grin off.'

Jake gave him a quick, angry look, but obeyed.

Caroline watched the taunting expression fade from his eyes and found it easier to relate to him while he assumed the sombre stare which matched the black wig he wore as Napoleon. He strode across the set, his head set belligerently, caught her shoulders and kissed her. She reacted in a surge of fear, struggling. 'Good,' said Paddy.

Jake was not taken in, however. His eyes held an angry glint as he looked down at her, and when he began to undress her she knew he was doing so pleasurably, his eyes filled with a glittering enjoyment, quite deliberately handling her body as much as possible. Paddy seemed well satisfied with the scene and when it was finished they were all sent home.

Jake drove her back to the flat in silence, whistling, glancing at her with a curious little smile from time to time. When they were in the flat Caroline turned on him angrily. 'It can stop right now, Jake, or I walk out on the whole series!'

He assumed bewilderment. 'What do you mean?'

'You enjoyed yourself a little too much today,' she said.

He smiled sarcastically. 'When I take your clothes off, Caro, I'll do without an audience.'

'I'm never going to bed with you, Jake,' she said flatly.

'Wait till you're asked,' he snapped back, flushing.

'We both know what this is about,' she said. 'Your pricked ego! You set out to have fun with me today. You took those clothes off with a grin from ear to ear.'

'Why the hell shouldn't I?' he asked. 'It's not often you get paid for doing something you've wanted to do for a long time.'

'I ought to have slapped your face,' she said, fuming.

His face altered. 'Caro, darling ...'

'No,' she said. 'Jake, I love you dearly, I always have. I always will. I'll admit, I was tempted ... for a little while. But it would never work, Jake. Don't you see? We're not matched.'

'We are,' he said earnestly, coming closer. 'Darling, we are.'

She shook her head. 'You and Maggie mean a lot to me. But if we were all in a balloon with James and only two could stay, I know who I'd push out.'

He gave a sharp crack of laughter. 'Caro, the things you say!' His mouth turned down and he sighed. 'So it's still James.'

'It always will be,' she said. 'I'm crazy about him.'

He stared at her in silence, then said lightly, 'That's that, then.'

CHAPTER NINE

AFTER that Caroline found herself slipping easily into the old, warm close relationship to Jake. The disturbing intimacy vanished again. Jake had accepted that there would never be anything else between them but friendship, and as she had suspected, although he had not been easy to convince, once he was convinced he accepted it with the shrug of resignation she had known he would give.

At times it occurred to her that had she never met James she might well have drifted into marriage with Jake—or at least some relationship akin to it. And that, she thought wryly, would have been a mistake, because although they cared for each other the profound emotion she felt for James did not enter into her feelings for Jake, or, she was sure, his feelings for her.

Jake had unbalanced her briefly when he made love to her. She had felt the pull of his attraction and she was aware that she felt it even now. Jake was a very attractive man. The attraction was purely reflex, though, an instinctive feminine reaction to physical allure. During those moments in his arms she had let her mind be silent, but as soon as she saw James again her whole personality began to clamour, because with James it was body, mind and spirit which were involved, not merely the body.

She missed James badly. At night she clung to her pillow, fretting for him, and she several times came close to ringing him or turning up at court again, but some instinct made her stay away.

Maggie's friend Rob had turned up again. Caroline liked him on sight. He was a quiet, humorous Scot with a peak of rough hair and a grin which substituted for words, with which, as Maggie had said, he was sparing. Seeing him with Maggie, Caroline was convinced he loved her, but he was not hurrying into matrimony. He had a cautious look about him, and although he watched Maggie's

lively antics with a smile, she sensed he was not
certain they would make a good pair.

Several times they made up a foursome for dinner.
Maggie had not given up her matchmaking. Caroline had told her firmly that there was nothing between herself and Jake but friendship, but Maggie
was stubborn and Jake meant a good deal to her,
although she occasionally burst out with irritated
words about his arrogant opinion of himself.

'If the big star is ready ...' she would snap, and
Jake would give her his most annoying lazy smile,
mocking her.

'Maggie resents my success,' he told Caroline.

'No! There isn't a jealous bone in her body.'

'Jealous?' Jake considered the word. 'No, that's
true, it isn't that simple. Maggie feels I may leave
her behind, forget her, move off into the wide blue
yonder.'

That sounded more like it, because Maggie had
that fighting tribal spirit; she wanted to preserve
their triangle of friendship eternally, she did not
like to see it splitting up.

'She's very fond of you,' Caroline said.

'Of both of us,' he substituted.

She nodded. Maggie had never become a great
success. She worked often enough to make her career
a quiet success story, but she did not have it in her
to shoot to the top, she was not ambitious enough.

'In time,' Jake said thoughtfully, 'she'll marry
her Rob and settle down to raise a family.'

Caroline envied Maggie that possibility. She
yearned to have a baby even now. She was drawn to
prams, enchanted by the sight of tiny hands and
feet, the warm, soft helpless look of small children.

Jake gave her a long look. 'So will you, I suppose ... if you and your James ever get around to it,
if he can spare the time from clawing his way to the
judge's bench.' He grimaced. 'I'll be the only one of
us left in the business.'

'Funny that,' she said. 'You were the one of us
who never took it very seriously, always playing the
fool, chucking your chances away.'

'Yes,' he said, looking at her. 'Well put, Caro.'

She was uneasy under his eyes. 'You've redeemed
yourself now, though ... it's been a pleasure to work
with you, Jake. I've learnt a lot from you.'

'Glad to be of service,' he said lightly.

It was true. She had been impressed by the
quality of his acting, by the sheer hard grind he put
into achieving what on screen promised to be a
superb performance. She had watched him building
it up piece by piece and he had surprised her.

'Don't give up your career yet,' he told her, suddenly serious. 'Your marriage can wait a while. Caro,
you have talent. Don't waste it.'

'I won't,' she promised.

When their studio scenes were finished, the rest
of the cast were moving off to Spain to shoot the
location work. Paddy took her aside at the end, to
congratulate her and kiss her warmly. 'I'm pleased
with it,' he said, which was obvious to her, because
when Paddy was not pleased his eyes glowed like an
angry bull's and he got a savage sound to his tongue.
'I'd like to work with you again. Keep in touch.
Who is your agent?'

'Jake,' she said, laughing, and Paddy gave her a
strange, quick look.

'You and Jake are ... ?' He ended discreetly with a smile and she shook her head.

'Friends,' she corrected. 'Old, dear friends.'

Paddy looked down his nose. 'Ah!'

She knew he was not convinced. Everyone on the set had been sure that she and Jake were lovers: their eyes, their voices, their looks had made that obvious from the start. The other men had left her strictly alone, not wishing to tread on Jake's toes. He was already someone to reckon with, a star with a long reach.

'Well, if I ever have anything for you, I'll find you,' Paddy told her, and she thanked him.

'A celebratory dinner,' Maggie said happily.

'No,' said Rob. 'I've got tickets for that play I did the sets for.'

'Just us, then,' Jake said lightly, and Maggie and Rob exchanged looks which Caroline saw with rueful understanding.

Jake would be away for months shooting the main part of the series. There would be hundreds of extras, largely recruited on the spot, because they would be making the battle scenes and they would need two armies of extras. It would be a far more arduous part of the filming, much of it shot long-distance, with tiny snippets of scenes sandwiched between the endless shots of men fighting.

'I'll miss you,' he said over dinner, pouring wine, his eyes on her glass, not on her.

'You'll be too busy.'

He smiled, lifting his eyes in a wry gesture. 'Okay, Caro.'

She flushed, looking quickly away, and he reached

over the table and took up her hand, playing with her fingers.

'You haven't found anything else yet?'

'Not yet.'

'You will,' he said. 'Don't lose heart.'

'I saw the agent you recommended ... he was hopeful.'

'Good,' he said, and she wondered how much talking he had put in on her behalf before she saw the man.

'I wonder if I could make it on my own,' she mused aloud, frowning.

'Of course you can,' he said.

She looked at him directly. 'Then let me, Jake.'

He flushed and grimaced. 'What do you mean? I got you the audition with Paddy. You got yourself the job.'

'After you'd twisted his arm a bit,' she said.

'Darling,' he protested, 'Paddy wouldn't stand for it.'

'From you he might,' she said.

'Let's change the subject,' he said.

'Why?' she demanded, bristling.

'Because,' he said carefully, arranging his wine glass with a bent head, 'if you don't I might go quietly out of my mind and say a few things you won't want to hear, Caroline.'

She was still, staring at him, frowning. Jake lifted his head and looked at her briefly. The look in his eyes made her look away.

There was a silence, then he said lightly, 'When I get back I'll expect to hear you've been working flat-out and making yourself a name.'

'As the best parlourmaid in the business, probably,' she said in the same voice. 'I played the part so often during rep.'

'Maggie and I thought you did a lovely Nina,' he said, and she sighed, remembering the production of *The Seagull* in which she had played the sensitive part of the lost girl.

'The only good part I ever had.'

'There'll be others,' he said reassuringly.

They talked easily after that and when they rose to go Jake guided her with an arm around her waist, his hand lightly resting below her breast.

Coming into the restaurant was a figure whom she recognised with a sickening leap of the heart. Jake saw him at the same time and his hand dropped from her waist, but James had already seen it, and his blank, cold features warned her as much. She braced herself to speak to him, but he was turning and speaking to someone, his black head glittering under the lights. Jake had halted, but now he moved on, his hand going back around her waist, tighter this time, holding her, as though he were afraid she might be unable to walk alone.

She looked past James and saw the woman with him with sharp, angry eyes. As she and Jake approached them the blue eyes went to Jake in surprise and amusement.

'Darling, you here again! It's a long time since I saw you. Is this your favourite restaurant?'

'Decidedly,' smiled Jake, retaining Caroline in the circle of his arm.

Simone looked at her past him and smiled with wry amusement. 'Well, well, well!' She looked from Caroline to James, her brows arching quizzically.

Caroline was staring at him, willing him to look at her. He turned the shaft of his grey eyes on her slowly, with open reluctance.

'Hallo, James,' she said.

He nodded, mouth straightening, then he took Simone's arm. 'We're late, I'm afraid ... excuse us, will you?'

Jake looked down at Caroline outside. She was standing on the pavement in the cold night air with no clear idea of how she had got there.

'Are you all right?' He looked worried, supporting her.

She felt as if she were slipping away from him, slowly sliding down against her body, and her hands clung to him to hold on to something real.

'Caro?' Jake sounded far away, his voice booming as though it came from under the sea. She remembered as a child listening to the sound of the sea in a sea shell and wondering what it felt like to drown. Now she knew, and it was distinctly unpleasant. She struggled against it, her skin chilly, and felt her body suddenly weightless. She was floating in air and she tried to open her eyes, but the weight of her lids was too heavy.

She slowly surfaced and found herself in Jake's car, the night air rushing over her face. He was driving beside her and when she stirred he said quickly, 'Lie still. I'm getting you to a doctor.'

'I'm all right now,' she said, half sitting up.

'You're still seeing a doctor,' he said.

'No, Jake,' she insisted. 'It was the shock.'

His jaw tightened. 'I gathered that ... I wish I'd punched the cold devil in the face!'

She laughed. 'I wish you had,' she said. It would

have brought James out of his icy withdrawal, but then he might have killed Jake. Jake did not know the depth of hatred James felt for him.

'Take me to the flat,' she begged, and Jake reluctantly agreed. He would not leave her, however, he took her inside and made her lie down on the couch while he made her some tea which he oversweetened and made disgusting.

'Ugh!' she said, grimacing.

'Drink it,' he ordered. 'It will help the shock.'

'Old wives' tale,' she muttered.

'Drink it,' he insisted, so she did, slowly, with sickened distaste. Jake crouched beside her, rubbing her cold hands, his face worried.

'I'm fine,' she said, forcing a smile. 'I'll get off to bed. Thank you for everything, Jake. Have a good time in Spain.'

'I'm not leaving you like this,' he said.

'You are,' she nodded.

'No, Caro. I'll wait until Maggie gets back.'

'That could be hours,' she said. 'You've got an early flight in the morning.'

'Who cares? I'm not leaving you alone tonight.'

He was immovable on the subject, so she left him in the sitting-room and trailed into her bedroom. Slowly she got ready for bed and slid into it, putting out the light. She lay there, worrying about Jake. He would be fit for nothing in the morning if he got no sleep. She got up and went into the sitting-room again, blinking in the light. He got up and looked at her quickly, then away again.

'Why don't you sleep on the couch if you won't go home? At least you might get some rest.'

'Very well,' he said, nodding. 'Now go back to

bed, Caro, before my animal instincts get the better of me.'

She flushed under those derisive eyes and backed. Jake laughed, but beneath the mockery she saw no true amusement. As she closed the door his face sobered and she was disturbed by the expression in his eyes as he watched her.

She went to the window and stood there, staring out into the dark street, consumed with anxiety about Jake. She heard him moving about, then the light went out in the sitting-room and she heard him settle on the couch, moving about restlessly. She stared at the wind-troubled sky with unseeing eyes, frowning, then her eyes caught a movement in the street below and she glanced downwards.

A man emerged from the shadows and stood staring at the windows of Maggie's flat. With a leap of the pulses she recognised James and her body tensed in delight and hope, then she saw him turn his head to stare at Jake's car, parked outside.

'Oh, God!' she whispered huskily.

James looked up again, thrust his hands into his pockets and turned and walked away.

Caroline ran from the room and Jake sat up in the darkness, asking anxiously, 'What's wrong?'

She did not stop to explain. She ran out of the flat and tore down the stairs to the street, tripping over her nightgown hem, shivering in the cold night air.

She looked down the street with terrified eyes, but James had gone. There was no sign of him. She ran down the road, unconscious of her half-dressed state, his name on her lips.

'Caro, for God's sake!' Jake caught her, pulled

her into his arms, anxiety on his face. 'What the hell do you think you're doing?'

'James,' she babbled. 'James ...'

He swore under his breath. 'You're delirious ... I knew I should have got that doctor.'

'No,' she muttered, struggling against his arms. 'He was here ... I saw him. He saw your car. The lights. God, what he must be thinking! I must find him, tell him ...'

'Darling, you're not dressed for rushing around in the street in the middle of the night. Come inside. You're freezing. You'll catch pneumonia.'

'No, Jake, I must find him!'

'Later,' he said, lifting her up into his arms as if she were a fractious child. 'I'll find him for you, Caro.'

'You don't understand ...'

'Yes, yes,' he soothed. 'Don't fret about him. I'll sort it out for you.'

Caroline struggled helplessly. He carried her back into the flat and put her into bed while she fought against his hands. 'Keep still, my darling,' he said huskily, frowning.

Weariness came over her and she lay back, eyes closed, a tear squeezing out from beneath her lids.

'That's better,' he said, smoothing back her tumbled hair. 'Just lie still for a while.'

A short time later a doctor bent over her and she looked at him dazedly, blinking in the light. He examined her and was very gentle. 'It might be the start of something,' he said aside to Jake, his tone just audible to her. 'I've no idea. No symptoms to point to anything in particular. Just keep her in bed and watch her. If she starts to run a temperature give me a ring ... sleep may be all she needs.'

When he had gone, Jake came back to her and sat on the side of the bed, looking at her kindly. 'Try to sleep, darling.'

'Find James,' she said wildly. 'Jake, tell him it isn't true.'

'What isn't?' he asked in that gentle, soothing voice.

It was no use—she saw that. James would not believe a word Jake said. Circumstantial evidence. She said it aloud and Jake frowned at her. 'What?'

'Nothing,' she said, closing her eyes again with a sigh. 'I'll go to sleep, Jake.'

'That's it,' he said, stroking her hair back from her cold face. 'Go to sleep, my darling.'

She woke up and found Maggie looking at her in a daylit room, her face concerned. Bleakly Caroline looked back. 'Hallo, Maggie.'

'How do you feel now?'

'Fine,' said Caroline.

'You look terrible. Jake said you fainted, were delirious.'

Caroline asked, 'Did he get his flight?'

'He wanted to get a later one,' Maggie told her. 'But Paddy insisted on dragging him off to get it.'

'I'm glad he didn't miss the flight.'

'Caroline, what happened?' Maggie leant over her, frowning. 'Jake was in quite a state. He was worried about you. He didn't want to go.'

'I'm fine,' said Caroline, feeling horribly sick. She slid out of the bed, swayed, her skin dewed with chill perspiration, and then gave a gulp and ran to the bathroom.

Maggie wiped her face afterwards with a damp

sponge. 'Caro, what can be wrong with you? It must be a bug.'

'Gastric 'flu, probably,' Caroline said, shuddering. 'I feel terrible.'

She went back to bed, but the sickness abated and she felt well enough to get up during the day. Maggie protested, but all the symptoms had gone. She was fine for the whole afternoon, although at Maggie's insistence she went to bed early that evening.

In the morning she was sick again. Maggie was disturbed enough to call the doctor. He arrived and asked some brief, impersonal questions. Caroline answered, feeling suddenly shaky with a totally new suspicion.

The doctor read her expression. 'Could it be, Mrs Fox?' he asked drily.

'Yes.' She was trembling and he saw it.

'You aren't pleased? You seem worried.'

She swallowed, eyes moving away from him. 'I ... I would be very happy, doctor, but my husband doesn't want children.'

'That's a pity,' he said, staring at her. A faint embarrassment touched his face. 'It ... it is ... ?'

She caught the intonation and laughed a little wildly. 'Oh, it is my husband's child, yes ... that wouldn't make any difference.'

When he had gone she sat and stared at nothing for a long time. Maggie came in and they looked at each other in silence.

'Are you going to tell him?'

'No,' Caroline said suddenly, her mind made up. 'I ... couldn't go through all that again. I want this baby.'

'How will you manage?' Maggie bit her lip. 'Oh, I'd be only too happy to let you stay here rent-free, but babies are expensive ... you would need medical treatment, baby clothes. You have to live, Caroline.'

'There's my allowance,' she said, calculating quickly. 'I could work for some time.'

'Not,' Maggie said drily, 'on the stage.'

Caroline laughed at that, but the amusement soon left her face as she contemplated the ways and means of it. 'But I'll manage,' she said firmly.

'You've no family to help, have you?' Maggie sighed. Caroline's parents had been middle-aged when she was born, dying during her years at drama school, one within a few months of the other.

'An aunt in Cardiff,' she said. 'I've only met her twice. I can't even remember her name.'

'James has no family?'

'None.' Caroline grimaced. 'Oh, distant relatives, like me ... aunts and uncles he barely knows ... but we had that much in common, we were both orphans.' It had contributed to her isolation, that lack of family support.

Maggie glanced at her secretively. 'There's Jake,' she began, and Caroline threw her an angry, commanding look.

'You're not to tell him! I forbid it! Maggie, promise me ... this is nothing to do with Jake.'

Maggie looked obstinate. 'He asked me to let him know how you were,' she said. 'I promised to write regularly.'

'Promise me you won't tell him a word about the baby,' Caroline said firmly.

'I think you're a fool,' Maggie burst out. 'Jake

would want to help ... when he finds out I lied to him he'll be furious.'

'I'll explain it to him when I see him,' Caroline said. 'I'm not Jake's responsibility, Maggie.'

'He thinks you are,' Maggie muttered, sulkily.

Caroline ignored that: she had to. There was only one thing she could do about Jake and that was to pretend blindness now.

A week later she got another television part, a few fine lines in a first-class play by a modern writer, and Maggie was exultant. 'You're having luck? That's a real break.' Her face sobered. 'Until ...'

'Until I have to stop work,' Caroline said drily. 'But not for a few months yet, thank God.'

She was ten weeks pregnant if her guesswork was accurate. She had not noticed the first symptom which should have alerted her to her condition. She had been too disturbed over James, too keyed up over the TV series. Now she had worked backwards and decided it had happened on the day she went back to their house to pack. It seemed ironic that she should have conceived from that bitter explosion of barbaric jealousy. She could have wished for happier circumstances, but whatever the cause, she wanted this baby too much to care.

The days and weeks went by very slowly. She had to abandon all thought of work as her body altered shape and her pregnancy became obvious. 'A shame,' the agent said, sighing. 'We were getting some interest.' He looked down. 'When is Jake coming back?'

She flushed, seeing that he imagined Jake to be the father.

'I've no idea,' she said angrily. 'Good day!'

Jake had rung several times, but she had always contrived to be otherwise engaged. Maggie had tried to persuade her to speak to him and she had refused. 'He's suspicious,' Maggie said, and Caroline shook her head.

'No, just string him along.'

Maggie had told him Caroline was getting work. He had been pleased, Maggie said reproachfully, giving her a sad look.

In the flat Caroline pored over the knitting patterns Maggie had found for her. The minute garments she was attempting to make seemed too small to fit anything, and she laughed to herself as she cast on the first stitches. Only yesterday the doctor had told her she was past the danger period. The middle months of her pregnancy should be carefree, he implied, and she thought of the increasing difficulty she was having with clothes, the heaviness of her body. Carefree? How like a man!

Someone rang the door bell and she waddled to open it feeling like a duck, her back aching after the long walk back from the agent's office. She had started walking to save bus and taxi fares. It was good for her and it saved money. She was still insisting on paying Maggie the rent, but she worried about her allowance. It was not elastic.

She opened the door and froze, shocked. 'James!'

He stared at her as if his eyes were deceiving him, and in that moment she felt fear and alarm. Instinctively she tried to close the door again and he jammed it with his body, forcing his way past her.

She shrank and his white face took on terrifying anger. 'My God, what do you imagine I'm going to do to you, Caroline? What sort of monster do you think I am?'

Why was he here? she asked herself, staring at him. 'What do you want, James?' she asked, impelling her voice to come, and it was hard because her throat was dry with nerves. It was worse than stage fright. She was trembling.

'Is it mine?' he asked abruptly.

'Yes,' she said, fury in her face. 'Yes, James!'

He closed his eyes briefly. 'I wasn't sure.'

She turned away. 'You'd better go ... there's nothing to say.'

'Leave you like this? You're not having my baby in a tiny London flat on a few pounds a week!'

'The baby is my problem,' she said angrily.

'Ours,' he said tightly.

'No,' she insisted. 'You don't want it!'

'I want you,' he muttered in a hoarse, thickened voice. 'Why do you think I'm here?'

'No,' she protested. 'I couldn't bear it. I want my baby surrounded with love, not jealousy.'

James winced and sat down suddenly, his hands over his face. His fingers were shaking and she stood there, not knowing what to do. 'This time it will be different,' he said through his muffling hands. 'I swear it ... darling, let me look after you. You can't go through this on your own. You need me.'

'I always have,' she said, and he dropped his hands and looked at her passionately.

'I love you. Don't send me away.'

She was crying. She couldn't stop the tears. Because she did need him and yet she was frightened of the future. James stood up and put an arm round her slowly, as if afraid she would push him away,

then as she turned her face into his shoulder his
other arm came round her convulsively and he
buried his face in her hair, kissing it, murmuring
her name softly.

'I'll make it work,' he told her huskily. 'I swear
it, Caro.'

She put both arms around his body, under his
jacket, her hands feeling the warmth of his body
gratefully, stroking the strong back. 'Just hold me,'
she whispered.

His arms tightened and they stood there, pressed
together for a long time, not speaking, merely needing the closeness and security of each other's body.

'Redway rang me,' James told her later, sitting
beside her on the couch holding both her hands.

She was astonished. 'Jake did?'

'From Spain,' he said. 'The line was appalling.'
He smiled wryly at her. 'I barely understood a word
he said, but the general drift got over.'

She was staring at him with a frown. 'What did he
say?'

'He told me you needed me,' James said. His
mouth took on a crooked humour. 'When I'd
stopped cursing him, I listened ... he said you
weren't well, weren't working ... he sounded worried.'

Had Maggie broken her promise, after all? Caroline suspected it. James looked at her frowning face,
his eyes bleak. 'I had to come,' he said. 'But I never
suspected this.' He looked away. 'I thought you and
he ...' He broke off and she watched his face closely,
trying to read his mind. 'I came round here one
night and he was here all night ... I saw his car outside.'

He was not looking at her, his eyes averted.

'I was ill,' she explained. 'Jake slept on the couch. Maggie wasn't here and he wouldn't leave me alone. He thought I was feverish, he called a doctor.' She had left out having seen James. She did not think she was up to a long explanation.

James let out a long sigh. 'I see.'

'You do believe me?' Her voice shook because she was so afraid he doubted her explanation.

'Oh, yes,' he said, and her eyes betrayed her surprise.

He lifted her hands to his mouth, kissing them passionately. 'Caro, when Redway rang me he said a few things which made everything look quite different.'

'What did he say?' she asked, eyes curious.

James gave her a quick, secretive look. 'Does it matter?'

'If Jake told you something which could have that effect, yes, I'd say it matters.'

'He made it clear that I had nothing to fear from him,' he told her huskily.

'I told you that.'

'You didn't tell me that he would cut my throat with a blunt knife if he thought you would ever forgive him.'

'Jake said that?' She laughed and James looked at her strangely.

'He said that,' he agreed, and Caroline thought it was funny and sounded like Jake at his most whimsical, but James was not laughing. He was looking at her with a wry sort of expression. 'I found we had a lot in common,' he told her.

'You and Jake?' She could not believe it, her

green eyes stunned. But whatever Jake had said, it seemed to have worked. James was here and she sensed a change in him and she said, 'I could kiss Jake!'

'Over my dead body,' James said.

'It would have to be,' she agreed, smiling at him. 'I love you quite ridiculously, do you know that?'

'So Redway said.'

She was stung. 'Did you have to wait for him to tell you that?'

'I've never been able to believe you cared for me the way I care for you,' he said, but the bitterness had gone, he was smiling, the handsome face softened, the grey eyes brilliant with passion. 'From the day we met you seemed out of my reach, even after we were married, like some exquisite butterfly always evading my hands, and I was afraid I'd go mad and grab at you, trying to hold you, only to crush you.'

'I'm tougher than I look.'

'You needed to be,' he said drily. 'I'll make it up to you, darling. It will be different now that I'm sure you aren't hankering secretly for him.'

She wondered again what exactly Jake had told him, but she decided it would be wiser not to ask too many questions. He was here, and she needed him too much to risk losing him now.

'You will come back to me?' he asked her, brushing back her hair from her face with a tenderness he had never shown her before.

'Me and the baby,' she said, because she wanted him to think what he was taking on, she wanted him to accept the baby.

'You and my baby,' he said, the possessive pronoun making clear his total acceptance.

She smiled with relief and love, then looked round as Maggie burst in upon them, scowling. 'Are you all right, Caro?' All her tribal instincts were rising to the fight and she looked at James aggressively.

'I'm going home,' Caroline told her, smiling, because Maggie cared what happened to her and that was what mattered most.

'Oh, Caro!' Maggie looked irate, incredulous, but she had too much common sense not to know that Caroline needed her husband now, and it was his baby, so she merely looked on with wrath as they packed Caroline's case and said goodbye. 'I'll let Jake know,' she said as they went, and it was a threat. James gave her a dry look, his face at its most sardonic. 'He knows,' he said, and it silenced Maggie. She was open-mouthed as they drove away.

'What did Jake say?' Caro was bursting with curiosity. She had to ask after all.

'That I was a fool,' James said. 'And my God, he was right!'

CHAPTER TEN

'I'M going to have to answer a few probing questions in the village,' Caroline told James next morning as they sat over a late breakfast.

'I don't see why,' he said flatly. 'Neither of us have been here. They won't be aware that we ever separated.'

That surprised her. 'They don't know?'

Shaking his head, he explained, 'I took a flat in London.'

Caroline gave him a quick, curious look. 'And dined with film stars?'

James laughed, his grey eyes amused. 'Did that make you furious? Simone was dying to ask me questions, but she was very discreet.'

Simone had some idea of how things were, Caroline thought, but aloud she asked, 'Did you fancy her?' And her tone wasn't altogether light.

'Would you mind if I had?' He wasn't looking at her.

'I'd scratch your eyes out,' she said frankly.

He grinned. 'She is pretty special.'

She dug her nails into his wrist, making a little growling noise. 'Watch yourself!'

It was the first time she had ever dared make a mock jealous scene and James looked at her with smiling eyes.

'It did occur to me to drive out fire with fire,' he admitted.

'What's that supposed to mean?'

'I thought I should broaden my horizons a little,' he told her teasingly.

'Forget me with other women?' The thought of that had occurred to her several times in the past months and she had not liked it: her tone admitted as much. 'And did you?'

He pushed a wandering lock of hair back from her face. 'No,' he said, looking at her in a way which was very convincing. 'It was never really on the cards. You're like ivy, Caro ... you cling.'

'Even to your granite nature,' she teased.

'Especially to that,' he said with a sober ring to his voice. 'I can't get you out of my heart.'

'I won't go even if you try,' she promised, and heard his deep sigh.

'I'll hold you to that,' he told her.

She looked down at herself with a wry face. 'Even if you turn off me when I'm the size of a balloon?'

He laughed. 'It suits you,' he said. 'Gives you a very permanent look.'

'God, I hope not,' she exclaimed. 'I would hate to look like this permanently.'

'At least no other man is likely to steal you while you're that shape,' he said teasingly. 'Maybe I should have kept you pregnant ever since our marriage. Why didn't that occur to me?'

Caroline was amazed that he could joke about it and it seemed to her a very good sign. His long secrecy about his jealousy seemed over and now that it was out in the open, a subject for jokes, it might be on the way to being cured.

He returned to work next day, but he had organ-
ised Mrs Carter as a baby-sitter for her, refusing to
leave her on her own in the house. 'I've months to
go yet,' Caroline had protested, but he was adamant.

'I want to know you're safe when I leave you,' he
said.

She took walks down to the village every day,
meeting her friends, talking to them, finding their
household preoccupations more enthralling now
that she herself was about to have a child. They were
full of chat about pregnancy and she learned to turn
a deaf ear to the bits she did not care for, the worrying bits.

'Take no notice,' Jean said comfortingly. 'You're
very healthy. No reason why you should have a bad
time. Some women love to exaggerate the problems.'

The months seemed endless to her while she
waited for the baby. James was quite different now.
Caroline found it an easy matter to talk to him, as
though some great stone had rolled away between
them. The one thing that worried her was how he
would react to the birth of the child. She was afraid
he would resent the intrusion of a third between
them.

Whatever Jake had said to him had altered him.
He was calmer, more approachable, more openly
loving. The brutal passion of his lovemaking had
become a tender affection which she relied upon
more and more.

As the days to the birth approached their climax
she found time went slower and slower. She began
clock-watching, finger-counting. 'Only six days and
then . . .'

'It could be overdue,' warned Bob, grinning.

'Not James's son,' she said.

'And it could be a girl,' he pointed out.

Caroline shook her head. 'James will want a boy.'

'He'll want what he gets,' said Bob. 'And so will you.'

'No taking back if the sex is wrong?' she teased.

'Definitely not,' Bob grinned.

In the end the baby came in the middle of the night, waking her from a restless sleep with a pain which made her yelp and grab James with both hands.

'Darling!' He sat up, grey with alarm.

'Bob,' she muttered. 'Get Bob ...'

'I'll ring the hospital,' said James, patting her arm.

She realised then what the pain meant. 'It's coming ... James!' He was dialling but she moaned for him, panic in her voice. 'James!'

He came back to her, having finished his brief conversation, and put both arms round her, and she leaned her bulky shape against him with a long sigh.

'Stay with me. I need you.'

But in the hospital they dismissed him to the waiting-room while Caroline was ferried away, abandoned to the brisk hands of nurses and mid-wives, her eyes turned back to him pleadingly as she vanished.

'A girl,' they told her some hours later, although it seemed like centuries to her and she was exhausted.

'A girl ...' she murmured, looking at the crumpled, squawling object they offered her. The little eyelids flicked back in a way which was oddly familiar and James's eyes looked at her, blue and deep on the child, but set like his under dark brows and in a face which already looked to her Celtic.

'A long skinny girl,' the midwife said, smiling.

When James came in to see her, she was already half asleep, her face drained against the high pillows. He held her hand, looking down at her with a smile in the grey eyes, and she struggled against the weariness which was engulfing her.

'Have you seen her?' She heard her own voice whispering, the sound thread-like, and tried to smile, but her mouth was so tired.

'Yes,' he said huskily. He lifted her hand to his mouth, kissing her fingers one by one, his face tender. 'Darling, you look so tired.'

'Yes,' she said, closing her eyes, because she was afraid. He seemed indifferent to the baby, and Caroline desperately wanted him to love her. How could he sound so cool confronted with that tiny scrap who already bore his stamp upon her flesh?

'Have you thought of a name?' he asked, still playing with her fingers. 'What about Madeleine? That's a pretty name.' He laughed softly and her eyes opened in surprise. 'All that black hair on such a small head,' he said. 'She looks like a mop. Did you look at her fingernails? They're perfect.'

Caroline stared at him, holding her breath. He talked, stroking her palm with one finger, and she saw that he had noticed every detail of the baby. He talked of her toes, her eyelashes, her ears, as though he were amazed to find she had such things.

When he had gone, Caroline slept for hours,

utterly content. She had been afraid he would not
want a daughter, somehow expecting him to prefer
a son, but now she saw that his whole nature in-
clined him to look on a daughter with fascinated
adoration. He would be a doting father.

Her room next day was a bower of flowers. She
scolded James when he came in, shaking her head
over the expense, and he laughed, shrugging with
amusement. 'You deserve it ... how is Madeleine
today? Can I see her? I went out and bought her
some toys yesterday ... a white fur rabbit four feet
high ... wait till you see him!'

She watched him with smiling eyes. 'James, she's
too young for toys.'

'Oh, but I want her to grow up surrounded with
pretty things,' he said seriously. 'While you're in
here I'm having the spare room decorated. White
paint and nursery transfers, I thought.'

The nurse came in, beaming from ear to ear,
carrying a silver woven basket of dark red roses,
dozens of them, it seemed, the dew still shimmering
on their damask petals. Caroline groaned. 'Oh,
James! How extravagant of you! I'm already knee-
deep in flowers.'

The nurse arranged them by the bed and went
out, grinning, but James said quietly, 'Not my
flowers, Caro.'

She looked at him, biting her lip.

He bent and pulled a card from among them and
handed it to her with a blank expression. She slowly
looked at it and her hands trembled. James took the
card back and glanced at it.

There was no name on it. Just three words. 'To
my love,' James read aloud expressionlessly. 'He

must have wired them. He's still in Spain.'

Caroline looked at him nervously. 'How do you know that?'

'I rang him last night,' James said, and she was so surprised her eyes flew open to their limit, her lashes fluttering.

James looked at her, his austerely featured face calm. 'I had to tell him you were all right. I knew he'd be waiting to hear.'

She looked down, fiddling with the lace strings of her bedjacket, her fingers trembling. 'That was kind of you.'

'I owed him something,' said James. Then he laughed. 'To be frank, I had to talk to somebody about Madeleine ... I can't think of another soul in this world who would be as interested in her as Redway, and I needed to talk. I described her to him and he said she sounded fantastic and he couldn't wait to see her.'

Caroline could not take her eyes from his face. 'That's nice,' she said faintly, wondering if her eyes and ears were deceiving her, and this was not James talking so easily about ringing Jake and giving him a long description of Madeleine.

'A funny thing happened to me when I saw her,' he said softly. 'I discovered that love is like the amoeba—divide it, and it multiplies, the more you stretch love, the further it goes ... it's elastic stuff.'

Tears came into her eyes. 'I know.'

James looked down at the card still in his hand. 'All the same,' he added drily, 'he can stop that sort of thing.' And he tore the card up, which made her laugh huskily. 'I'm not giving him carte blanche to bombard you with love letters,' he said, looking at

her through his dark lashes with a glint in his eyes.
'Fellow feeling has some limit.'

When he drove her and the baby home from the
hospital, she was amused and surprised to find that
he had taken time off to furnish the new nursery
with an array of expensive, enchanting toys; pandas,
bears, furry animals, arranged around the room on
deep shelves. A coloured mobile of butterflies hung
on a string over the white cot.

'Won't that make her squint?' she asked dubi-
ously.

'No, no,' he said in total seriousness. 'It helps
them to focus at an early age, but I've arranged it at
the right distance, anyway.'

'You sound very knowledgeable,' she said, laughing.

'I got a book on it,' he said sheepishly, producing
a paperback. 'I thought I should find out how to be
a good father. After all, bringing up a child isn't
easy.'

'No,' she said solemnly, eyeing him with loving
amusement.

'We must do things the right way,' he said.

'Yes, James,' she said, stroking his hard cheek.

Mrs Carter came into the room and cooed over
the cot, touching the baby's petal cheek with one
finger. 'Isn't she a love? And who looks like their
daddy? Look at that black hair!'

'Look at that nose,' said Caroline teasingly, eyeing James. 'Poor mite!'

James pinched her ear. 'What's wrong with her
nose? A very pretty nose, in my opinion.'

'Because it comes from you,' Caroline mocked.
'What looks fine on a man is going to look very odd

on a little girl!' His arrogant, Roman nose had too much masculine hauteur to fit well on a small female face.

Mrs Carter bustled off and Caroline sat down on the low wicker nursery chair, opening her dress. 'Time for her feed. Hand her to me, James.'

He carried the baby to her, then sat down beside them on the floor, propping himself up with his hands. 'Can I watch?'

She laughed. 'It's not a sideshow!'

The baby fastened its tiny black head with a struggling, starving movement, the tiny hand patting her breast rhythmically. Caroline inhaled as she felt the needle-like pain of the first moment. James was staring, riveted, fascinated. 'Good lord,' he said, watching as his daughter's skin turned pink under her black hair with the sheer lust of her pleasure. 'She's the greediest thing I've ever seen!'

'She enjoys herself,' Caroline agreed, grinning.

'I can't blame her,' he said, and their eyes met. Caroline blushed and laughed.

'Let me,' he said, as she switched the baby to the other breast. His fingers delicately took her nipple and the baby's mouth hungrily assaulted it, eyes closed. James did not remove his hand. It slid smoothly over the white skin, caressing it, his eyes on the baby's blind, absorbing face.

'Sheer unadulterated will to survive,' he muttered. 'In such a tiny object, too. Incredible!'

'It's the life instinct,' said Caroline, nodding.

'You're essential to her, have you ever thought of that?' he asked soberly. Then he looked at her, his eyes passionate. 'You're necessary to both of us.'

'And you to me,' she said gently.

'Am I, Caro?' His grey eyes rested on her face, their hunger as naked as that on the face of the child.

'Yes,' she said, touching his cheek with her hand. 'Oh, yes, James ... didn't you know?'

Harlequin Presents...

The books that let you escape into the wonderful world of romance! Trips to exotic places... interesting plots... meeting memorable people... the excitement of love.... These are integral parts of Harlequin Presents— the heartwarming novels read by women everywhere.

Many early issues are now available. Choose from this great selection!

Choose from this list of Harlequin Presents editions